Matthew Herbert is a prolific and award-winning composer, artist, producer, DJ and writer whose range of innovative work extends from numerous albums to film scores and installations, as well as music for the theatre, nightclubs, TV, games and radio. He has performed all around the world from the Sydney Opera House to the Hollywood Bowl. He is director of the new BBC Radiophonic Workshop, an artistic researcher in the School of Music and Performing Arts at Canterbury Christ Church University, and has a PhD in the ethics of composing with sound. Matthew Herbert lives on the marshes in East Kent.

The Music

An Album in Words

Matthew Herbert

unbound

First published in 2018

This paperback edition first published in 2022

Unbound

Level 1, Devonshire House, One Mayfair Place, London, W1J 8AJ

www.unbound.com

Produced in partnership with Whitstable Biennale

Typesetting by Bracketpress

A CIP record for this book is available from the British Library

ISBN 978-1-80018-154-0 (trade pbk)
ISBN 978-1-78352-507-2 (trade hbk)
ISBN 978-1-78352-508-9 (ebook)
ISBN 978-1-78352-514-0 (limited edition)

Printed in Great Britain by Clays Ltd, Elcograf S.p.A

1 2 3 4 5 6 7 8 9

For Hamza

Contents

What follows takes place over a one-hour period.
Every sound is possible.

I

Prelude

It's
three-thirty in the morning and
we're far underground in one
of the deepest
trenches
of
the
Pacific
Ocean.
A
hole
has
been
drilled
down
through
the
ocean
floor
and
a
small
microphone
has
been
fed
through
the
hole
some
considerable
distance

vertically downwards.

We are listening to huge plates shift subtly, but on a colossal scale. Slowly we fade up a hydrophone attached to a weight resting on the sea bed. We hear an echo of a long reverberant but distant boom. Then, nearer the surface, a thud on the bottom of a submarine. An identical boom again back down below. Further up, a string of bubbles.

Behind another vessel, the one that is recording what follows, there is attached a substantial length of cable. Along its line, at long but evenly spaced intervals, there are twelve waterproof speakers. As the vessel rises to the surface, slowly towing the speakers, the ocean-floor hydrophone records the following sounds, one sound per speaker, in slow succession:

A man asleep in Denver.

A girl asleep in Chibok.

A woman asleep in Monklands.

A man asleep in Sydney.

A woman asleep in Guangdong.

A parent asleep in Gaza.

A woman asleep in Uppsala.

A doctor asleep in Quetta.

A man asleep in Al Wakrah.

A person asleep in Kent.

A family asleep, on the move.

Something away

from

the

earth,

awake,

listening.

1.

Andante

To move

It starts with a single dry sound, no reverb. It's the sound of this book opening slowly in the late morning, quietly though, as if read in private in a dark corner. The paper subtly creaks as the spine separates and opens. A tiny buzz from a nearby table lamp is the underscore. The crease of the paper on the first page-turn mixes with the wet ping and dry crackle of wood on a fire. Once the page-turn is finished, there is a too-soon silence. Within that void you can hear your own breath bristling against the hairs on the inside of your nose as you exhale. There are two of these exhalations but on the third a surprise: a recording of a strong January wind catching the remaining winter leaves of four old oak trees artificially planted in a row. The sound is contained, though, as if through double glazing. This wind fades up over a minute, slowly evolving, the higher frequencies filtered out in a slow sweep as we become aware of a tone that simultaneously contains a hum, a whine, a throb – the lonely, dull drama of a Boeing 777 at night.

Riding above it is the snore of a white, fifty-year-old American male asleep in first class on an Emirates flight to Dubai. He snores at a similar pace to your own breathing through your nose. Now a 'fasten seat belt' alert sounds. After a pause, it is chopped up and repeated quietly at different pitches. Its rhythm ducks and twists its way round the sound of the manmade fibres of the carpet as they rub against the soles of air stewards' shoes as they make their way through the sleeping cabin. The pace of the crew matches the snore of the man. Someone else is hurriedly stepping aboard the rear section of an articulated bus in Basel and their footsteps merge with, and then are interrupted by, a shrill, dense cacophony of 1,129 alarm clocks belonging to garment workers going off at once in Bangladesh. The alarms are recorded separately in their bedrooms but overlaid upon each other. The recordings are placed in a room-simulation reverb, mapped from inside Philip Green's most expensive car. Over the tail of these brash sounds fading out, we hear the tiny sound of someone putting in a disposable contact lens, then a child on a bike setting off down a hill, then a car with blacked-out windows pulling up to a border and then a petrol tanker glancing its wing mirror off a rusty drainpipe in Sabaneta. The driver gets out of the truck and as he slams the door, the alarms stop in unison and we hear the dust and gravel scatter round his worn suede boots. He walks towards the boundary-type microphone lying flat on the ground. A crescendo, a rising of different lifts and escalators in government buildings, a small cluster of seatbelt-sign sounds from different flights. He stops. A hood slides clumsily over someone's head. A soda can drops from a vending machine. The winding of a watch. Curtains are pulled back. One by one, in quick, rhythmic succession, there is now the slamming-shut of truck doors from every country in the world, forming a fierce pattern some way between a samba and a glitchy beat from an early-1990s circuit-bent drum machine. We sometimes hear the backgrounds to these slams too: a cockroach scuttle in Guadalajara, a smeared call of a bird of prey mid-swoop, a checkpoint in Riyadh, breaking glass, a blur and tangle of five motorway service stations in Germany, Austria, Poland, France, Belgium. As they come to the end, we hear a warning klaxon on an aircraft carrier and then a blizzard of spot-welds recorded at the MINI factory in Oxford, precisely ordered at a rapid tempo. One weld for every new car made since the Kyoto Protocol was signed. A slowing down, a dry pumping of feet on bike pedals and then, in miniature fractions, we hear hard rain splitting on a mechanic's roof in Colombo. Thunder overhead. A van full of empty Nestlé water dispensers goes too fast round a roundabout and they tumble around in the back. A sudden gush of spray off a ship's bow. The secret flush of a train toilet. A historic water mill slowly turning but doing nothing.

From this lull, the irregular throb of the main road from Moscow to Kiev at night. People everywhere are tiptoeing up flights of stairs in the dark. Men are gently moving pianos in broad daylight. Armed robbers are climbing casually into the back of getaway vehicles. Taxis are pulling slowly in to hotel forecourts. Elsewhere a civic parade is starting, but there's no music yet, just flatbed trucks with generators and elaborate fake scenery, and people walking and dancing in step behind the floats to keep warm. A drone by a prison jerkily takes off. An ambulance rushes through traffic, in the back an imminent birth. All the cars on the school run, sped up drastically into a curt, deathly buzz. The snap of a lid on a Tupperware lunchbox. Jeans are hurriedly pulled on at dawn. The screech of metal beneath trains. A family is leaping from a boat onto rocks. A cat knocks a broom over. Someone bangs their head on a low wooden beam in an English pub. A child's bare thigh down a slide. A carpenter turns on a circular saw. A large group of cyclists is just about to pull away from traffic lights in a city. A transporter is overturning on a country road, spilling broken wind-turbine blades across a field.

Over the top of this plastic, aluminium and steel is laced a delicate prickle of water drops from the bottom of a just-watered hanging basket of petunias into a rusty tin bath on a crisp morning in a Chadlington garden. They have such a clear pitch, it could be the sound of glass. Through these sharpened drips is woven a searing melody, skewed and burned out by amplified distortion and metal-plate reverbs to resemble music for a sunset. This melody sounds like the cry of some mistaken, misc-Asian folk instrument, but it's made from the squeal of the brakes on the cream-coloured Mercedes taxi that picks up another half-asleep white American male from the airport. We hear it in its raw form as the phrase falls, muddier now beneath the wheels of Asian-made carry-on suit-cases leaving over the roughed-up mats by the automatic doors exiting customs. We hear the rasp of these rolling wheels in brisk, perky grinds before being swept up in a rising pitched-up swoop of military planes on takeoff until we find ourselves listening to the dry sound of 35 to 135 doors opening in Coventry and Dresden alternating in each ear. This is doubled up with the repeated slap of failed skateboard tricks on a Nissan Qashqai TV advertising shoot. A model NASA rocket takes off abruptly and its whoosh ends just in time for the final drip of water to hit the Chadlington bath, resonating and reverberating onwards.

Our American's carry-on bag has a fake-leather detail on it which is now rubbing against the black, piecemeal, composite leather of the rear seat in the taxi as it bumps and turns, each disturbance progressively louder. The rubbing is at the same tempo as the truck doors but doesn't quite fit with the aircraft engine – he is already out of sync. But there are still uneven moments of silence between squeaks, moments that are filled with a waiter coughing while on his lunch break, a waiter the American once overtipped in Café de Flore in Paris in 1998. The brakes squeal in a long slow-down as the taxi overshoots the red traffic light and the aircraft engine disappears within it. A miner sneezes.

Now the hurried shuffle of four people into a lift as the doors close. A bolus squeezes through an oesophagus. A husband and wife – a pair of Chinese cocklers – rush back to a minibus. Someone drags a dining table across a carpet. An air-traffic controller grabs a printed strip of a flight number in a control tower. The plastic grasp-handles creak and strain on a full Tokyo subway train. A Chinese satellite-launch vehicle fires up. The roar of a race car across a desert. Two-and-a-half thousand coffee-shop workers unknowingly bang out grinds in unison. The brisk click and flip of wooden geisha sandals on tarmac. Five hundred and forty-eight train tickets are hastily clipped. The clapper on the bell prepares to strike on Dublin harbour lighthouse. A loud bang as a worker empties a portafilter at an AMT coffee outlet in Chicago airport. Hundreds of thousands of people empty their pockets into plastic trays. Bottles of water tumble from plastic crates. A thousand cardboard boxes drop into the back of a thousand removals lorries. A million automated passenger gates open. A rising shimmer and gurgle of hundreds of people cleaning their teeth in bathrooms in public places. It becomes intense, overwhelming almost. Then they all come to an end at about the same time. A slither, a smeared shuddering of teeth and spit and taps and hand dryers and children. The driver gets back in his truck and slams the door behind him.

A dog pulls its owner along through a park; it is damp underfoot. A crow at the side of a road taps on a piece of rotten bark. Someone tears open the paper backing from a packet of AA batteries. A father is blowing on damp tinder by a newly set fire by some trees in the hope that it catches. A teenager is cutting something out of a magazine with scissors in the back of a camper-van in a layby. Someone is listening to a recording of plane turbulence on headphones on a stationary tube train. A child is tying a shoelace – we hear it in close-up. A car-parts delivery van idles in a layby. Parents are arriving at a school concert. Two brothers run through a forest in the distance.

Inside the cab, the truck driver taps his as-yet-unlit cigarette on the back of the packet. A regular part of the tapping becomes a loop: soft, familiar, enticing, but a little menacing after a while. The almost inaudible friction between stone chippings in a pave-ment as a sea-cadet marching band walks over them. The rolling wheels of 1,800 buggies, pushchairs and prams while the children inside are asleep. In the distance a night train passes quietly over points on its way through the Alps. People are licking stamps, but we probably don't hear it. We do hear for certain the subsonic booms recorded from a boat across the estuary from Shoeburyness in quick succession. They loop and become a huge rounded warm boom, a structure on which to measure everything that follows. And then the upwards whine from an aeroplane's engine as it ramps back up, ready to move on to its next destination.

Now, the propeller of the *Queen Mary* as it leaves New York recorded from underwater. The grind of a bulldozer heading towards a wall, recorded from the wrong side. The steam of a coffee machine on the lower deck of a tourist barge. The meowing of two distant quad bikes chasing through the pattern of poplar trees across a field in summertime, the leaves shudder-ing in the breeze. A tank lumbers through Fallujah; a tank is accelerating in Afghanistan. Startled birds fly up out of heather and gorse. A clap to indicate someone should start running. But instead, a single step from John Major in the Houses of Parliament. A single step from someone towards a noose. A single step of someone onto the set of a TV show. A single first step out of hospital on crutches. A single step onto an iced river. A single step into a tent in a refugee camp. A single step on grass at some important football match in Dortmund. A single step onto the tail of a cat. A single first step by a toddler in Syria. A step towards a lover. A single heel on an unwashed marble floor. A single muddy boot on the steel floor of a cabin atop the tallest crane above São Paolo. A single step backwards from an approaching bear. A single tiptoed step in a Greek tax office at midnight. A tentative first step on skates to a roller disco. A step to the urinal by Paul Singer. A step into the branch of Pret A Manger on The Cut. A step in the dark by a lake. A step towards an unknown judge. A step up an ill-set ladder. A step towards an unknown shape by the waves. A boggy step through marshland. A step onto a landmine. A step onto a stage. A step forward through dark rock and dripping water in blackness. A step on a just-mopped floor. A step in snow, exhausted. A step, a step, a step. A boom from Shoeburyness at the same time as our truck doors close together again. Another flight lands in Dubai at the same time as a cathode-ray TV set powers up in a prison about to show *Days of Thunder*, one TV turned up in a different prison, one turned down. One plane up. One TV down. The poplar trees shudder, the tin bath is emptied down a grate, spliced into the demonic sucking of the uneven drains in the British Airways First lounge showers at Heathrow Terminal 5. We just listen to the horror of the sound as it gets louder and louder, this bizarre squelchy sucking noise that sounds so alien.

A load of cutlery lands in a drawer at the same time; it's later, darker. An unripe lemon falls off a conveyor belt. A woman drinking lemonade on a bus is reading a magazine article about David Oluwale. A mouse or a rat is hidden in a wall, scurrying up and down in bursts. In the gaps between the rat we hear a car horn in the distance. Someone is indicating something, but it's not clear yet. All we know is that unedited, it falls exactly in the gaps of the rat journeying down the wall. The running of young children at the gates of a Catholic school in Jakarta. A crab scrabbles, stuck in a plastic bucket with no water. A red-faced woman jogging too fast with headphones on. The car horn fades up. As it gets louder, more horns. A funfair is arriving in town on the back of trucks. A military parade is setting off in the distance. Phones going off next to kettles boiling. All the climbers clipping on ropes and carabiners on the sides of mountains. All the wind heard rushing through spinning spokes, through railings on boats, through computer fans. The sound of all hot air balloons rising. All canoes down rapids, all motorbikes overtaking, all ships setting sail. All the helicopters taking off, recorded from above. All the mopeds pulling out, recorded from underneath. Now the ooze of Canadian tar sands.

Now the muddied sound, recorded from inside, of a hundred male commuters' hands randomly thudding on a metal handrail at a London station recorded from the inside of the rail itself. One commuter's hand creates a particularly long bong on the rail that resonates languidly and painfully. The sound is fed back through empty sections of the keystone pipeline with a ribbon microphone and some huge speakers, creating a howl of lugubrious bloom, a purity of tone that baffles and booms and slips and terrifies and tips and excites and punishes and leaps and rewards and scares and grows and grows and grows and rises and leaps and blooms and blooms and overwhelms and at its peak stops dead with a short break followed by a thud: a suddenly headless pigeon has fallen out of a tree and hit the tarmac by your feet next to a front gate on Tankerton Road. The sound is like nothing you have heard: a mixture of feather, and guts, and air, and dust and cedar needles. A whoomph, like a central-heating boiler firing up. But there's a thwack to it too, as if someone punched a hollow wall with a thick cushion over their hand. There may be other birds still heard in the background, and there's no sign of the head, but you don't notice either of these things. You notice how recent the blood is, though. It should have never happened, but it did. And it can be heard here.

2.

Adagio

To wait

A schoolgirl with black hair, dirty shoes and a short scar on her arm is sitting on the end of an unmade bed at dusk with headphones on. We hear the tinniness of the sound for a while as it leaks from her ears, but it's impossible for us to work out what it is. There is a slight breeze through an open window. An occasional insect, the angry bark of a stray dog.

We crossfade into a different sound – 180,000 hotel mini-bar refrigerators, many of them empty, grimly buzzing in unison. It takes ten minutes for the sound to rise up slowly, as if distilled through a filter that only allows lower frequencies. A man is playing the recording of these fridges from a set of speakers somewhere outside Los Angeles, in a semi-desert area, and we're hearing it from the perspective of a shotgun microphone held by a woman carried towards the speakers on another woman's back. The sound of the fridges has been carefully put together according to the star rating of the hotel system, with the lowest-rated hotel fridges heard at the start. The fridge sound is stacked as the hotel rating gets bigger. The five-star hotel fridges are the last ones we hear and are likely to be quieter than many of the others – the world gets quieter the richer you are. We may hear a little dust kicked up along the way, or a light aircraft overhead.

Just as the sound of the fridges becomes overwhelming, intense, it cuts suddenly to the inside of an empty shipping container inside a depot at night in an unknown Chinese port. We think the container is empty but again, slowly rising over twenty-three seconds, we hear the sound of every black prisoner in America breathing in unison. This is played out of a mobile phone left on a bright-green plastic seat.

Over the top of these two long recordings, we start to hear layered sounds. An overhead projector on full in an empty board-room. A bleep of a cash machine. A slow knock. A different room tone – an air conditioner is positioned some distance from our vantage point, but its grey wind and greyer noise can be heard through a small grille in the ceiling of the room. Someone has knocked again on a neighbour's door with three quick knocks in succession, but there's no reply and it's not clear if the person who knocked has left yet or is waiting there. There appears to be no sound from inside. In fact there is someone in the room, and there's a microphone very near their head. We can tell from their breathing that the person is not asleep. There is an anxiety in the unevenness of the breath and we hear their mouth open a little after the third inhalation. There is a slight crisp brush as their head tilts a little on the stiff cotton of the pillowcase. We carry on hearing that, but underneath there is now the slight rustle of thirty to forty people of mixed ages trying to be still, in a different kind of space, a presence. After thirty seconds or so of this, a rhythm fades in of a chugging air valve on a recently empty beer keg in the basement of the Queen's Head pub in Downe. Beneath it, the tone of an empty, windowless bathroom. People are staring in silence up at the departures board in a train station. A knock. Many people are ringing a loved one but their call isn't being answered. A life jacket is thrown towards a dinghy. New recruits at a call centre sit in silence as they wait for the supervisor to arrive. Another knock. We then hear all the different ringing tones from around the world. They are layered and organised so that the person who is holding the longest is the last call that we hear. At the exact point the caller hangs up, a huge metal urn for heating water has been turned on by someone a long way from home. The bubbling is layered up underneath what follows, but it never reaches a peak, we never hear the urn switch off. Instead it fades out slowly over two to three minutes. By the time it has gone, you won't have noticed. You may hear the sound of your own clothes as you shift your position instead.

The girl slowly turns the handle of a roughly painted wooden door.

A dog is scratching the closed door to a flower shop. A few musicians turn the pages of their newspapers over as they wait for a studio session to start. A cook is filing his nails with an emery board next to a pan full of hot oil in a prison kitchen, but it's not at temperature yet. A page of scribbled notes is torn from a book. The doors release on a Eurostar train with a tough exhalation of hydraulics. Seventeen washing machines in seventeen women's refuges have finished their cycle but they haven't been emptied; we can hear the last of the water draining away. A bath is run but nobody is in it – we just hear a dripping tap. A doorman is gently kicking a brick wall to keep his toes warm. Trainee priests are practising swinging incense at the same pace. Tourists are queuing up to use a bathroom near the Egyptian Pyramids. The watch of a waitress is ticking furiously in Istanbul – a microphone has been set in her sleeve. A teenage boy in black is walking towards his school with a variety of weapons in his bag. The slipping of thick lenses into testing glasses at an opticians. A huge but quiet crowd looks around nervously. Every time someone opens a back door, the wind passes through the ground floor of a hotel in Kampala and the fronds of a plastic palm tree in the lobby rub against themselves. An elderly man is yawning by a fence at night. The snap as someone stands on a twig.

All the hotel TVs on standby in Korea buzz together for a minute. A text message is received at a bus stop. A scientist's shoulder clicks as she bends over in a yoga class. A traffic warden writes out a parking ticket. A person working on the front desk of a hotel listens to the scratching of the pen of the overweight guest filling in the form and then there's a tight click as one hundred credit cards are put on ninety-nine countertops. Now a firm yank on a ticket from a machine that gives you a place in a queue at an embassy. A traffic jam in a New Jersey tunnel. A spy in a hotel room with headphones on absentmindedly fiddles with a Hot Wheels toy car. A woman on hold to a bailiff quickly presses her phone to her ear in such a way that we hear it click against her earring.

A child on a boat yawns. Another child is sleeping nearby. Another child's teeth are chattering very slightly behind the first child. A child is standing in the dark at the top of the stairs shaking, their bare feet nudging the same spot on a cold floor. A child is inside an ice-cream freezer, but we just hear the hum of the refrigeration unit. A child is on a bike at traffic lights, playing with their brake lever in time with a child 1,000 miles away on a rooftop picking at moss with a toothpick, in time with a child not so far away shaking a bag of Lego, in time with a child running a metal file along their teeth, in time with a child dragging a stick down the side of an expensive car, in time with a child a long way from all the others brushing dust off their trousers. We hear a child in a hiding place waiting to be found.

While on a phone call, someone is absentmindedly stroking an expensive sculpture in the shape of a giant bench made out of disposable electric toothbrushes, the bristles facing outwards, but it gives the illusion of naturalness from the sound it produces.

A sharper sound breaks this new spell: a bag of frozen peas being thrown into a freezer. Now the ineffectual scraping of ice off the inside of a window with a passport. A collection of microphones set in seawater listening to the freezing over of winter but sped up like time-lapse. A bell as a bridge lowers in a snowstorm. Now ice being shovelled in one gesture in the Sydney fish market into a polystyrene fish box. Then the pumps in native oyster purification tanks inside a warehouse bubbling away. Another shovel of ice. More peas. Asma al-Assad is running a bath. A small brittle knock is heard if you listen carefully as she puts down a scented candle on the edge – the glass of the bottom of the candle touching the enamelled, metal bath. A shovel of salt. Someone is rolling up a prayer mat. A pedestrian crossing bleeps at night to indicate it's safe to cross. A maître d' is standing in an empty restaurant waiting for customers and looking down the road. A tour bus in Peru is being filled up with Chevron Diesel, a mic is placed in the fuel tank so we hear the fuel cascade in on top of us. We think it should sound like a waterfall, but it's an overbearing sound, reverberant inside the confines of the tank. We think we can smell it just because of the clarity in the mid-range of the recording. A shovel of American grain. A man with excellent teeth and hair is standing in a relatively fast-flowing river holding an empty net and a bent rod at the same time; we're hearing the net drag a little in the water. An unattended pot of grey water and bones is on a rolling boil on a portable gas stove somewhere hot. The file is edited so that we use the transient created by a small drop of liquid leaping from the pot and scald-hissing on the stove as the point at which we cut to the next sound. Ice shovelled. A queue has formed by a temporary cabin. A shovel of ice again. An approaching storm in Alaska recorded from inside a slowly filling community hall. Another bag of peas. An elderly woman with dark skin but pale hands is blowing on hot tea. A shovel of salt. The sound of running someone else's wound under water, hoping it isn't serious. A frozen packet of prawns thrown on the peas. Someone else is having a shower next door, but it's not clear from the sound whether the person has got under the flow of water yet. A shovel of ice into an ice bucket. The sewers beneath Fleet Street are moving freely down near Blackfriars Bridge. If the sound recording is long enough, you will also hear the blip of a gas-warning monitor hung around someone's neck. A huge reverb taken from a Catholic cathedral is added to this bleep, as if the sound nearly lasts forever. Another scoop of ice. Asma pulls down a blind over a window. Salt. A murder of crows in trees at dusk. Grain. Someone is applying makeup to a corpse to make it appear less pale. Ice. An original, antique, ornate Tuscan fountain now located far from Italy spits water erratically. An unaccompanied dog is licking an ice cream that has been dropped by a rubbish bin and is now rapidly melting. The first child on the boat is asleep now, but there are murmurings of adults over their breath. It's now low tide in the UK and we hear the delicate sound of trickling water and the ooze of mud sucking and drying. Actors are turning the pages of scripts as they wait for an audition. Someone is rolling a joint in a railway station quietly in the background.

The schoolgirl is anxiously washing her face as she looks in a cracked mirror.

A seat belt in the back of a minibus clicks into place. The dragging of chairs into a circle at an Alcoholics Anonymous meeting in Catford. A different seat-belt click. Someone is being tattooed right now with a corporate logo. Seat belt. The pulling down of a loft ladder. Seat belt. Any Austrian empty ski lift running today going down a hill ready to find someone to bring up to the top. A seat belt. Someone is hunched over a body waiting for an ambulance. Seat belt. A child in the back of a car on their own, licking their fingers anxiously. Seat belt. The chorus at the Royal Opera House whispering in the wings, about to come on. Seat belt. A far-right politician chewing gum. Seat belt. The small sound of scrolling downwards on a computer-mouse tracking ball, but the arrow icon is frozen on the screen. All the domestic ovens in France that are on right now. A seat belt set in the distant reverb of a cave. The light tapping of change inside a trouser pocket. Feet shuffle in a queue for Stonehenge. A policewoman on foot patrol catches the nylon straps of her bulletproof vest as she hooks her thumbs in. A meditation class stirs at the end of a session. A tiger is stepping through a forest; each paw placement we can hear is synced to a breath of a DJ waking up in a strange room abroad, unsure of where they are.

The turning of a pharmaceutical lobbyist's hard drive backing up a laptop.

Wind is blowing over the top of an abandoned Budweiser beer bottle on a beach near Aberdeen. This sound is sampled and turned into an eerie organ-like sound, played low and wide, its dense harmonies filling the lower end of the sound field until very nearly the end of the piece. A crackle of incense as it catches light. A bird swoops and lands on a traffic light turning orange in Tahrir Square. A geology graduate sucks milk through a straw on her lunch break until she reaches the bottom of the cup. A strong wind across unplanted fields inland. A TV newsreader shuffles their papers. Fumbling in the dark for a light switch. Bang – a hammer suddenly hits a nail in a shed by a railway track in the Punjab. In one speaker, a bug on a tree, in the other, the sound of a called hotel lift coming down from many storeys above. In the middle of the stereo image, the sound of someone sharpening a bayonet carefully, meticulously. Bang, the hammer again. Back to the lift, cicada, blade, elongated, stretched, the mix value on a reverb is moving from dry to wet, increasing the scale and width of the image; the whole thing sounds like it's slowing down, a pitch-shifter is moving down the scale in parallel, the sound glutinous and whole. Someone in uniform is sitting in the shade in an empty golf cart. Bang bang – hammering nails into cheap wood over a window somewhere in America. We hear the warning lights of all the cars sitting by the side of a road, broken down right now, recorded from the inside on a handheld recorder. Bang. A woman is playing with the seal of a Ziploc bag with her last few possessions inside. Bang. Men zipping up waterproof coats. Bang. Women praying in silence around a hospital bed. Bang. A stray dog panting. Bang. Someone is brushing a child's hair too slowly. Bang bang bang. All the office cleaners in the world's financial districts where it is early morning right now vacuuming the carpets. Someone else in uniform is sitting in the shade in a different empty golf cart 1,000 miles away. Bang. A power cut in Iraq. Bang. Someone has buried a sensitive mic in some fresh dough and we are listening to the dough rise in real time in the Azores in the heat. This could take many minutes, so we leave it running underneath the other sounds. We may hear some muffled, indistinguishable voices nearby from this mic buried inside the bread. Someone who helped make a pair of your shoes is in a queue to see a nurse. Someone else is in a bird hide, rummaging in nylon pockets. Someone else is cleaning an AK-47.

The girl hides behind a door, breathing quickly but quietly.

The patter of rain on a bald white man's head in Boston. A handful of gravel thrown at the window of a convenience store. There's the flapping of torn flags in the wind outside an abandoned Tunisian hotel. A doctor's coat is swinging wildly as they rush for shelter. Somewhere in the mix a shovel of ice again. A teenager is itching or scratching their recent chest hair. Seat belt. The buzz of batteries charging. Bang. Pumping up the tyres of a wheelchair at the same speed as someone digging a grave in the desert. Ice. With a microphone held incredibly close, we hear a young boy trying to read a map in the dark. Seat belt. A frantic woman is hurriedly pouring gurgling water into an overheated car radiator at a garage next to a highway. Ice. A thief is counting his money in a toilet cubicle in a McDonald's drive-through. Seatbelt. The ticking of a just-boiled, still-full kettle in an electrician's Portakabin. A plastic England flag attached to a car's wing mirror whips against itself as the car snakes onto a ferry. Chinese concrete settling, hardening. The click of another seat belt. A pig's-fat candle spluttering. Bang. Someone is holding someone else's hand in the back of an ambulance, but it's the siren we hear. Bang, an animal headbutts a cage. A woman who cooks gyoza at Kameido in Tokyo is listening on headphones to a YouTube video about treatment for burns. A photographer is loading a film into a Nikon F4 camera in Malawi. A girl is trying to keep herself warm on her first porn shoot. The safety catch is released from several guns in several places right now in real time. An out-of-work actor is having an AIDS test. Another person is alone in a van, the doors are closed and it's stationary with its engine off. A new printer cartridge is loading, the head whizzing back and forth. An immaculate general is flicking his lighter secretly in his pocket during a formal ceremony as people spin round him, refilling glasses with water from one-litre plastic bottles. Thousands of miles away, actors are rehearsing a play about the General's homeland and we hear the theatre lights clicking and buzzing. A mortar primed. A supervisor, stiff and uncompromising, comes towards us one step at a time. An electric gate to a private house in Hollywood opens. A crane winches a steel beam for an as-yet-unbuilt floor on a high-rise. Step. An empty, idling Range Rover and horsebox outside a post office. Step. A bully picking bits of twig out of his hair. Step. An artillery shell loaded. Step. A crowd of tourists hurry towards an exit. Step. A knock at the door. Step. The manager is coming closer towards you now. Step. A school-boy in Pakistan putting on his blazer and tie. Step. An overworked cooling fan whirring furiously on an abandoned Dell laptop in Tripoli. Step. A damp chestnut log spits in a fire in Powys. Step. A model-maker pinching two parts of a Messerschmitt's wing together until the glue dries. But the main thing we hear is his dog eating the man's leftovers in the background from an upturned tin helmet. Step. A hostage lying on the floor not wanting to get up. Step. The bleep of a photographer's camera locking focus on another body on the beach. Step. A combination safe being opened, recorded from the inside. Step. He's nearly here. Step. A roomful of children about to take exams but the clock hasn't been started yet. We hear their shoes knock lightly against the metal legs of their chairs. Step. A knot for a rope being tightened. Step. A boy pulls a gun from a backpack. Step. The scrape of pen to paper as a minister in London scribbles a doodle while on a phone call to someone in Saudi Arabia. Step. Stubble chafes against rope. The spring inside a long lever scrunches up in preparation for a release.

A queue for a rollercoaster temporarily goes silent. We listen to it for a while, wondering who is there and why they're not speaking. A tree whose top is impossible to see from on the ground starts to creak and swing precariously in a strong breeze. The beginnings of the movement of wet mud down a hill, the slide inevitable now. A teapot is sitting untouched next to a ticking radiator. A duck struggling to breathe is circling in a murky pond. Rain on the underside of an umbrella. A group of men are huddled in the corner of a rooftop, listening to sporadic gunfire. A thousand miles away, a surgeon in Valparaíso is stitching up a chest while tapping his feet coincidentally in time to a short burst of that same gunfire. In Ukraine there is the gentle rubbing together of warm, oily hands. And a librarian walking slowly down the corridor pushing a trolley of reports about Grassy Narrows over a dark green nylon carpet. Just as they are about to stop ... hot water tanks filling up in empty houses, overlaid with bubbles popping at the surface of a pan of warm custard in a campervan. An adult hand sifts through sand with their fingers spread a little apart. A child sits expectantly behind a closed door. A history graduate learning to drive waits at the traffic lights longer than necessary. In the background we can hear people pressing doorbells, buzzers, entryphones, knocking, trying to get an answer but with no luck. We hear them all beneath the idling engine of the driving instructor's car. A safety catch flicked off. A general's dog sniffing at a dark red puddle by the pavement. Above it a bee zips between two flowers. A gun cocked. Twelve boys fly down hills on eleven bikes, the freewheels on the rear wheel ticking furiously as they pick up speed. We can't hear it above the bikes, but underneath is mixed the sound of snow falling on the roof of a Koch Industries-owned cabin. The scrape of ice. A record-industry executive tips a ladle of water onto a sauna hot stone to make a loud hiss. The hiss blends with everyone whose net worth is over a million dollars and is heading for the bathroom right now. A pen top clicked. Supermarket workers, all women over the age of fifty, rubbing the tops of plastic carrier bags together in an attempt to get them open. Suddenly another step. The brittle sound of the supervisor walking towards us again. Step. The scrape of ice. The bang of an empty rubbish bin falling off a truck. A camera bleep. A hairdryer. More than one person somewhere is shaking a drink – vodka, maybe – to make sure it is mixed together properly. A louder step. A louder bang. A firm knock on the door. A child's first cry. Bright blue water is spilling over the top of a bath someone has forgotten to turn off. Windows are being wound up quickly, manually in an older vehicle. Flip-flops or sandals rushing down an echoey corridor recorded through a wall. It sounds damp. A huge crowd rises to its feet in silence.

The girl takes off her shoes and slowly ties them, along with some items, together in a bundle.

Pit mechanics at a race circuit are stirring sugar into their coffee. A soon-to-lose horse whinnies on the starting line of an inconsequential steeplechase. A paediatrician taps a syringe at the same speed that we heard the child's teeth rattling. A young man is sweating in a car with one finger tapping the steering wheel and another resting on a button strapped to his side. The kettle from earlier has a fault; it won't turn off and has now boiled itself dry and it's not stopping. A person sitting on a rock without any shade is wiping sweat from their eyes as they look behind and in front of them in quick succession. We've recorded this with a microphone right by the back of their neck. And so we can hear the dry skin as it twists a little in the movement, catching their collar. A lawyer is on a plastic chair listening to the buzz of the lighting above, also sweating. The CEO of a chemical company is straining on the toilet in a fancy restaurant. A child is making a prison out of Lego in the cold. A parent is reading a manual for a baby monitor while the baby is heard crying through the speaker. A car-company executive is drying their swimming shorts at high speed, high volume, in a special machine in the changing rooms of a Japanese hotel swimming pool. An uneven pump is helping a patient in a Gaza hospital to breathe. A series of bubbles from a small plastic pirate's chest in the bottom of an aquarium in a dentist's waiting room, recorded with a hydrophone, sped up, accelerating. A teenage boy is watching the first of the twin towers collapsing on an iPad with the sound down while he has his hair cut. A phone is ringing in a damp ditch near a car flipped upside down on its roof. Someone else in uniform is running down a jetty towards you. The jackets of several different people in different locations are flapping violently in the wind as their bodies fall at speed through the air. A coin suddenly falls from one of their pockets and hits the stones a fraction earlier than the sound that comes next.

A schoolgirl has her ear to a railway track, listening to the ping and whine of the metal as it shimmers, bends and readies itself for the arrival of the train. She gets up and starts running.

3.

Allegro

To hurt

Recorded from the inside, we hear the sound of every moving vehicle with four wheels or more headed for, or driving towards Berlin. It is an undulating river of drone and distortion. It starts in the distance, segued out of the previous track, and takes just under thirty-four seconds to reach its full intensity. There are no voices of passengers or drivers, or if there are, they are edited out. There is no music on the car radios and no traffic reports. There are just the sounds of engines, cars, tractors, trucks, roads, vans, motorhomes, ice-cream vans, pickups, sports cars. The occasional siren. We do hear the breathing of the people and everything that rattles or knocks inside the vehicles themselves. The recordings are organised in such a way that at precisely the same time we hear everyone arrive at once. They turn their engines off in perfect sync. In the distance we can just hear frogs at night in Khana like static.

The piece crossfades into someone else, in a different location, sitting alone inside their car with a brand new suitcase beside them, stationary, engine not running. A crudely bandaged hand rests on the steering wheel. They are at a junction in the road. There are few other cars around, if any. The landscape is flat. There is no wind. The sun is either rising or setting, but while recording, there will be sharp beams of sunshine cutting through the grime of the windscreen and filling the inside with light and shadows as we hear very soft nervous breathing, fast and even.

Quickly now, a meal dumped in a bin. Plates, glasses, cutlery. A door closes. Timberland boots on a wooden floor. A fire put out in a grate. A coin in an empty plastic charity box. A tabloid newspaper thrown on a sofa. The scrubbing of a stain in a bathroom.

The striking of a match. A knocking over of a teacup. A suede-effect cufflink box closes with a muffled snap. The tearing open of a crisp white envelope. A computer shut-down. A switch, any switch. The chopping of wood with a newly sharpened axe. A dog just locked in a cage. A key turn. A blade turning. A handle twisted left. A candle pinched out with wet fingers with a muted *phfft*. A hot pan plunged into cold water. A front door slammed.

We can now hear the creak of dry hands on a shiny, well-worn fake-leather steering wheel. Out of the creaking skin, the rattle of some coins in the tray, looped. The beat hasn't started yet. An empty drinks can briefly rolls round the floor, bashing into other cans that have been aggressively squeezed in half one-handed and thrown there. The clank becomes a vamp. The thonk of tyres on a four-wheel-drive SUV going over cats' eyes on the road to Greenham Common. This is the bit of the frequency range we usually assign to the bass drum, and here these thonks are edited, regardless of the fluctuations in speed, to a rigid 4/4 time signature. The interference on an AM radio in a caravan in Kinshasa no longer tuned to something provides a very quiet crackle beneath. The cranking of the musical energy pitches up and up until it's a tiny, high sound. The coins speed up their rattling as if accelerating or idling, but the tempo stays the same around them.

A single, blast. A long, all-enveloping held note from a car horn rises up artificially from the mix as we hear all the frequencies again. It's a late-nineties white Volvo estate parked in a driveway in the fog recorded at three in the morning blaring this single held tone. It's operated by an elderly man in a dressing gown and slippers. A phone keeps vibrating in a hitchhiker's pocket; she's sitting next to the driver of her first ride of the day. A Blaupunkt CD player is trying to read a CDR put in a retrofitted head unit in a Alpina E21 but struggling to do so, clicking and clicking and clicking, heard at the same time. The thonk continues; the layers stack up: a stray electric toothbrush has decided to turn itself on in the hold luggage of an Italian film student on a flight to São Paulo. It is amplified so it can be heard here. Above it, the sound of any UPS driver turning left. Now the overwhelming blast of every horn of every broken-down vehicle in India pressed and held at once. This continues for thirty-two seconds, then an abrupt end.

A pulling-on of tight medical gloves with a snap. A slop of a sponge into a bucket of warm sudsy water. A slap of a chamois leather onto a bumper. The squeak of a sponge against a windscreen as it wipes the blood off. A quick crackle and split of the opening of a black paper air freshener in the shape of a Christmas tree. The 'on' switch of a head torch. The slamming down of a bonnet at the side of a remote hillside track. A long hiss of air brakes on a truck carrying corn syrup as it pulls into a gas station. A yanking-on of a hundred handbrakes. The slot of a bulletproof electric window at a checkpoint as it pushes back into place. The bang of a burst tyre in a tyre shop as it's inflated too far by a young person in Fiji. The snap of a plastic wheel onto a model Hummel. The puff and squirt of the last glug from a plastic bottle of oil into an ambulance's engine. A child in a back seat is sick into an empty beige Christmas-pudding bowl. A snort of coke off a dashboard. A line-up of 2,020 vehicles from all around the world, having reversed up to a clearing in a forest and turned their in-car hi-fis on to play the same recording of traffic in Paris on Christmas Eve on a loop, but all starting at different times. It is a one-minute loop, and amplified so many times it becomes an indecipherable dirge. After four minutes it fades to almost nothing, just the sound of a woodland at dawn.

Someone bigger, in a different location, sitting alone inside someone else's car, stationary, engine running, their phone beside them. They are at a junction in the road. There are few other cars around, if any. The landscape is flat. There is no wind. The sun is either rising or setting, but while recording, there will be sharp beams of sunshine cutting through the clean glass of the windscreen and filling the inside with light and shadows as we hear very sharp, clear breathing, slow and even.

Again the shiffle-shuffle of hands on fake leather; this elongated but brief chirr forms the basis of a triplet loop across a mechanical

120 bpm. The backbone of the beat is a driver stamping in fear and anger on the footwell inside on the downbeat, and a different driver's wedding ring occasionally glancing on the hard brittle plastic of the gear lever on every off beat. On top of this, with no variation, no let up, no automation, no volume rides, no reverb, no EQ, no delay, no tricks, no stops, just raw recordings, trimmed in three-second batches, volume matched and at their original pitch: a red pencil snapped, the static of a walkie-talkie with little battery left, the bleep of phones running out of battery, the driving muddy rain on an asbestos cement-board roof, the tink, snap and metal tear of a ring-pull, a flick of a green BIC lighter, rosary beads knocking against the windscreen, a small bell from a Santa hat on the back seat as it rolls forward, the tearing-off of a taxi receipt, the manual winding-down of the window of a Trabant used in a radio drama called *The Unknown*, the rummaging in a thick coin-full wallet for change – a handful of rial, the squeaky wiping of mist from a windscreen by a chauffeur. The driving sand against the back window, the engine suddenly starts overheating. A thin black plastic belt unthreading from jeans. A locking of a bathroom door with gloves on. You start to realise a soft, blowing heater from a truck in Siberia is on underneath this all. Low, but on. The scrape of a credit card trying to clean mud off a car mirror. The heater is turned up a notch. Someone's stiletto heel on an empty cassette box in the footwell. Another click on the heater. A passenger's hair is rubbing against the window glass. Click. Teeth on a metal pole. Click to the heater's almost-hottest setting. A child in Yemen bangs their head on the underside of a school desk in the dark. The credit card snaps. A grinding click of the ashtray on a MINI. The wipers are on full now. The nail of a six-year-old boy down the ridges of an air vent. Shopping rolls out of the boot as the door is lifted. Someone pulls a tissue from the gilded box at the rear. A Caterham's indicator. A helmet bangs to one side on a roll cage. A pilot taps the lenses of his glasses as he takes aim. The heater clicks up to its full power. Then everyone in a taxi with a tissue box on the rear shelf takes one at the same time, but at that exact moment, a branch of a beech tree snaps off in the wind and drops on the deck of a wooden rowing boat in a storm. The beat stops.

The first driver in the stationary car with the engine off slumps forward and rests her head on the steering wheel.

An uneven idling – some kind of military tank made in a different country from the one where the tank is actually located and recorded. A shower turning on to disguise a noise we're not supposed to hear. The sound of policemen, one from each of the ex-Soviet states, tapping on car windows at the same time but played unedited at their original tempo. The touch of the wedding ring on the gear lever once more, and with that the stamping beat starts again but it's pitched up a semitone. The heater is still on full. A leather glove scrunches on a plastic steering wheel. A choke snaps back on an MGB. The flick of a finger as everyone in Munich turns the heaters on in their cars at the same time. Instead of the heaters, though, we hear a deathly chorus of all the air conditioning in Saudi. A door-slam of a Humvee, mixed underneath everything else; it repeats twelve times. Then from nowhere, breaking the beat again, uncompromisingly massive in the rich deadness of its sound, a rock smashes into the side of a bus. Three bullets through a car boot in quick succession; the blade on the left wiper needs changing. A single screech of a tyre that never stops. The crumple zone crumpling. The slice of a metal frame through a leg. The head again on a steering wheel. A shoe hits the back of a chair. A safety belt clicking into place. Everything in the boot shudders backwards. The impact of a head on the outside of a car door. That sound again. Again. Again. Again. Again. Again. Again. Again. Bits of glass from a window into a face. The head again. Tins of tuna from a bag of supermarket shopping are rolling around on the floor and bumping into each other – we think everything has stopped, but now a concrete block on a bonnet. An empty lorry into the back of an empty coach. A motorbike into a garden wall. Two vans into three trees. A car through the window of a tool shop. A lorry drives over a cyclist. A truck grinding down the side of a music-school wall. A mountain bike into another bike, a tangle of spokes. A car clips a ferry door at disembarkation. A limo driver opens a door onto a pizza moped. An oil tanker into the pillar of a bridge with a vast cracking sound. A broken bike wheel whizzing in a field. A car, going nowhere, is spinning around on its roof. A motorbike is on its side, moving still, scraping down the asphalt. A car driving at speed over an arm. A young head through a window. An even younger head hitting the roof. A handbag spilling its contents onto a dashboard. A wheelchair coming loose from its moorings in the back and hurling through the side-window glass with a National Trust sticker attached. A Luther Vandross cassette tape splintering inside a car stereo as it is crushed. The plastic of a child seat ramming against a portable DVD screen. A wheel over a hand that is wearing gold rings. A tooth through a lip. Steel against concrete. An eye out of its socket. A pair of Labradors crushed against a black metal dog guard. A maths student walks across a busy road looking down at their phone. Several simultaneous muffled screams inside Saydnaya prison. A scratched audiobook version of 1984 on CD is out of its case and rolling down an empty side pocket. A phone charger hacks lightly but quickly against the side of an ashtray full of gum. A slam of a motorbike and sidecar into a busy bus stop. A clang of steel into aluminium. The sludge of a wheel as it drops into a soft verge. A slop of blood onto blacked-out glass. A bike's front wheel bending sharply in two as it hits a pothole. A monster truck bursts in to flames. A blacktail deer onto the bonnet. A bang of a taxi into a pedestrian's legs. Pieces of metal scaffolding fall sideways off a transporter onto a convertible and tear its fabric in a swift rip. A wrecking ball through a living room. A head on the outside of a car door again. Again. Again. Again. A dead sound. Again. A hand coming away from an arm. A thighbone snapping. A fingernail pulled from a finger. Teeth grinding, then banging onto a wooden San Remo steering wheel, pushing them all out through the bottom of a jaw at once. A cocktail shaker. A fox's tail caught on a chrome bumper at night. A cry of pain surges in unison from inside two children's hospital wards a thousand miles apart. A series of cane toads under Australian wheels, skidding wildly at the same time. An in-car fire extinguisher explodes. A heavy book of out-of-date maps slides under the passenger seat and hits a small metal toolbox there. The clip of a wing mirror against a kebab-shop sign. An Amazon delivery van up an embankment into a stop sign with a ripping sound. A series of red bricks off a footbridge onto an unlit road. A £1m two-seater sports car into a guard rail at considerable speed. A plastic bumper ripped off in one hit. A tobacco tin pings against the brake pedal. Two wheels on the right-hand side of a coach on a narrow mountain road in South America leaving the road but still spinning. A beer bottle put down harshly by a driver before picking up keys. A short extract of sixteen cars sliding down separate hills backwards in the snow. The twang of metal as a safety railing snaps. A *whoomph* as petrol catches light. Twelve different side-lights on twelve different rocks. The whoosh of an empty rental car as it leaves a cliff at speed recorded from underneath the car with a Lomo shotgun mic. The high-pitched squeal of a brake pad looking for grip on a ceramic disc. The creak of a motor-caravan frame buckling. The crunk of the whole weight of a pickup truck onto the front springs. Some glass bottles dance loosely through the air. A splintering of bones. The rubbing of hair down textured plastic side-fill. The internal organs hitting a ribcage, recorded from the inside. The snapping-off of an indicator stalk and then the stump piercing a chest. A spare can of fuel flying overhead against the underside of a sunroof. A library book clips into a tree. The drip of blood from a nose onto an unopened sandwich pack. An ear into the rear-view mirror. A pelvis cracking. An unknown body coming the other way through glass. The rubbing of denim on tarmac in a skid and the grinding of metal studs on jeans on the tarmac. A collapsing of Ray-Bans into the cheekbone. The engine bolts shearing inside an engine. A series of wellington boots against a suitcase. The crushing of a radiator and the steam as it escapes. The pulling of cables from fuses. The pop of cheese and onion crisps beneath the weight of a body. The flutter of parking receipts meeting empty sweet tins in the background. A head against a door. A young head against a door. A younger head against a door. A door split. A door cracked. A door ripped off. Keys loudly jangling. Mints rattle in tins. Luggage falling out of racks onto backs below. A tree snapping underneath from the weight of a coach as it swings overhead. The tumble of bodies and chairs inside. The oil slopping about inside the engine. The squeezing, shattering of orange-plastic indicator lenses. The sound of a cigarette being put out on a tongue. Stiff tyres on runways. A Chinese truck head-on into an American truck. A train into a car that has stalled on a crossing. A VW Camper driving at speed over a body lying in the road in Johannesburg, recorded from inside the van. A Russian train's warning horn. A biting through the tongue. Hair pulled from the scalp. The unwitting chewing on gristle in a bar at an airport. A baseball bat to the kidneys. Someone opens champagne at a wake. The grinding of teeth again. The cut of a razor through skin and muscle. A smoke-ring blown by a doctor on a tea break at 2 a.m. A beard being roughly shaved off. An estate agent coughs. A scraping of matted hair. Millions of clicks of epinephrine auto-injectors. Rubber-gloved hands clapping quickly and quietly, trying to keep warm. A boulder on a neck. A limb tied to a car, dragging. A wig thrown on a fire. In the south, a crudely sealed clear-plastic tub of teeth, shaking. In the east, many people running down the outside stairs of housing estates and projects two at a time. In the north, the sharp poke of a dentist's endodontic tool into an infected gum. In the west, a fingernail being clipped too short as water is poured into a copper pot in the background. The dab of bad makeup. The short zip of a trouser fly, done by someone other than the wearer. A navel being pierced. An ear being stretched. A pair of hands, gripping a throat too tightly. A bull's horn through a hip. A heart into a polystyrene box of ice. A tumour placed in a steel bowl. A used bullet placed onto a glass counter. A squirt of air freshener. The locking of a small metal door. A bag thrown roughly at your feet. The clip of a crash helmet. A broken beer bottle jabbing in a face. A chainsaw through a leg. The air rushing out of a punctured tyre, elongated, stretched, examined, filtered, smeared, fragmented. The bursting of an eyeball. A pouring of milk into porcelain cups. The unzipping of a child's unused overnight bag. A text message from a phone on vibrate heard on a stainless-steel table. A single school bell placed in a huge reverberant space, a canyon or a vast cave. Shards of icicles drop onto rocks, all the low frequencies removed. Small stones pinging against windows sped up, pitched up, layered and overlapping. Tinfoil over a turkey. The rattle of partially built Windham weapons on a trolley in their factory. Someone at a wedding in Afghanistan is about to make a toast by tapping their knife on a glass. An ACADEMI executive is about to make a toast by tapping their fork on a glass. A car drives through a hedge at a car showroom. A tunnel collapses. An excerpt of an earthquake. A dam breaks. A waiter trips over a dog and drops a tray full of glasses and dirty cutlery. A Christian dives into a swimming pool on the top floor of a hotel. An elderly woman blinks in Niyeri. Knuckles into eye sockets. A blade through an organ in Dili. A shovel into earth. A single suck from a ventilator in a special-care unit for premature babies. An old man chokes. A pain-relief tablet drops into a glass of water. A nurse snaps a syringe into a holder attached to a metal stand on wheels while barrel bombs can be heard landing in the background. A blast of warm wind near the airport in Diego Garcia. A soft bell goes as someone opens a door. A car skids and swerves round a corner at some distance away from the microphone, but it becomes clear that it is travelling at considerable speed and is quickly getting closer. The snipping-off of the top of someone's ear. Nine hundred men shouting and running towards you.

A woman, bruised, sweating, sitting alone inside a car, stationary, engine not running. She is at a junction in the road. There are few other cars around, if any. The landscape is flat. There is no wind. The sun is either rising or setting, but while recording, there will be sharp beams of sunshine cutting through the grime of the windscreen and filling the inside with light and shadows as we hear slowing breathing, calm and desperate.

4.

Accelerando

To struggle

Two white men tipsy on Scotch whisky are driving a golf cart next to a sand dune. The sound fades in very slowly as they approach the microphone attached to the existing first flag. We will also hear the soft rhythm of waves from the sea and the occasional oystercatcher. As this recording reaches its peak and the golf cart is close, we suddenly hear the sound of a tall twenty-two-year-old man living in Yuendumu, his young daughter by his side, angrily kicking a slightly deflated leather football with a wide-sounding thwack. As the tail of the sound we hear all the helium escaping from punctured Disney balloons bought for children around the world. The ball begins to soar through the air.

A sonic bomb explodes in Syria.

Beneath the hum and churn of vibrating feeders on a machine for washing sand we hear nine imported cashmere goats in Afghanistan having their throats slit, one after another in quick succession, all at the same loud volume, all slightly sped up so that the sound goes past quickly. Somebody staples an invoice to an A4 photocopy. Snap – a mousetrap goes off. Crack – an egg from a battery chicken breaks on the floor of a hospital. Click – a hook snaps onto the belt of an engineer on the top floor of a skyscraper in Seattle. Crack – the snap of twenty-four chopsticks pulled apart in Japan. The bang of claws and feathers into metal as a peacock attacks its own reflection in the passenger door of a black car. The sizzle of a cow's rump being branded with a hot iron. A splitting-off of a huge slab of marble in a quarry. The messy clang of a handful of dead batteries into a steel dustbin. A large tree pulled over by a machine and chains with a series of birds' nests still in it. The snap of a packet of aspirin along a perforated line. A tractor's wheel driving over an organic yoghurt pot. A gardener unknowingly sticks a garden fork through a daffodil bulb. A pig electrocuted. We hear it thrash around until it's dead. A toilet won't stop flushing.

An empty plastic bottle of Evian on a beach in Ibiza is folded in half with a crumple pitched way down, so it feels like something large is toppling over.

A melodic arc, a long whine of whistles tied to the feet of pigeons in China recorded from a model aeroplane. Fading in, we hear the metallic harmonics of a shopping trolley in a river as water rushes through the wire mesh. Underneath we hear any feedback from microphones on stages right now, mixed extremely quietly. It slowly crossfades into a cello on fire in a cul-de-sac in Marseille, crackling in the heat as the lacquer melts and warps. The buzz of electric lines overhead in a national park recorded from a fibre-glass canoe. Beards being trimmed in Iceland. The spitting and spreading of salt from the back of a yellow lorry. All the hairdryers in Taiwan. Distantly, a tired fly bops against the window of a café. It's been doing this for some time and there are longish gaps as it stops, crawls, bops, stops.

After fifteen seconds or so the fly has some renewed energy and after a few intermittent fuzzy bumps into the glass, we hear a particularly loud one. At the same time we hear, through a micro-phone buried inside an anthill, the exact moment that a young boy jabs a stick in it. Some broken sheeting on scaffolding hiding a new coffee shop flaps viciously in a strong wind. A bonfire crackles with ivy as the smoke swirls. The furious noise of bees swarming round a beekeeper. An army helicopter appears suddenly over a headland, raising the volume and tempo again. All the sounds of drilling right now.

A dart misses a dartboard hung on a tree and sticks with a thwack into the trunk. A cat's paw on a crisp packet. An obese boy swings at a clownfish piñata with a stick. A bin bag full of disposable plates splits and spills over a lawn. Crack, a plastic surgeon breaks a patient's rib. A monkey lunges at bruised mangoes but a chain pulls it back with a sharp yank. A howl of pain from a fox in a trap by a railway bridge, then a snarl. A charity-branded promotional pen snapped.

A butcher in Malaga saws through a collarbone in a long, even motion. Over the top we hear acanthus-tree branches rubbing against each other in the breeze.

A pregnant woman is pouring water into a jug in Flint, Michigan. A handful of small river fish flap loosely but panicked in a plastic cooler. The crack of a water vole in a mole trap. A drip from a tap in an empty bathroom at the Mexican border. A shark bites through a surfboard. An excerpt of a jagged rockfall into a lake. An explosion. More rocks. Another explosion. Gravel rains down on reed roofs. The scoop of wet sand and grit onto the ramparts of a sandcastle. A dolphin bumps its head on the bottom of a wooden boat. A teenager throws a condom into a river in the dark with a pathetic splash. Two cans, one of varnish, one of paint, spill onto a canal path.

In quick succession: bang, a pigeon into a rooftop window on the left. Bang, a starling into a window on the right. Crunch, someone stands on a snail in bare feet. A sack of salmon-flavoured pet food dropped carelessly into the boot of a car. Someone stands on a mine. A vineyard sprayed with pesticide. A primate's head being shaved. A team of council leaf blowers. A bee buzzes next to your right ear, but you can't move. A wasp buzzes into your left ear, heading through the ear canal, further towards the eardrum. But now you're in a dark room that's not your own, next to someone snoring, and you can hear a mosquito above you. From nowhere we can hear many of the mosquitoes flying right now in Africa at once, millions of them, an orgy of tiny melodic humming and the friction of wings. It goes on for too long, maybe a minute in a crescendo. Then it snaps to silence.

Except we still hear one mosquito.

Someone cuts through a wasp's nest in a garden with an electric hedge trimmer. Now an explosion in a quarry recorded by a series of 1,549 microphones, each placed one metre back from the other in a straight line from the centre of the blast, radiating away from the central point. We hear each recording, one after the other, with a 0.43-second gap between them. The debris rains down in small dusty pellets. It morphs down the frequency spectrum, filtered until from the low end we hear a nuclear explosion in the Pacific Ocean, recorded underwater.

Someone throws a set of house keys into the sea from a ferry; we hear it as a kind of arc. Fifty-six thousand footballs forcefully kicked.

The *thunk* of a poison dart in the side of a chimpanzee. The hum of fridges, machines, fans, fluorescent tubes beneath the scratching of mice in laboratories against the plastic walls. A tortoise on the floor tries to free itself from underneath a skiing jacket where it has got trapped upside down. This merges with a furious bug trapped in a beer glass on a picnic bench in summer, which in turn merges with a rhino's tusk being sawed off. A shepherd bashes the head of a lamb with a sharp rock. The fly-tipping of a fridge. A professor washes her hair vigorously with lavender-scented shampoo; a tree in Borneo collapses. The tumbling of carpet rolls from a lorry. A bodybuilder is sucking up spiders and ladybirds with a vacuum cleaner. A distant car bomb recorded from a mountain. A father is blowing up a balloon for a baby shower.

From inside a Toyota Land Cruiser now, we hear a sandstorm – the pelt of sand against the metal and glass. Commercial European printers are rapidly printing out books about trees. Circular saws are spinning as people lay decking in their gardens. Every fly approaching a bug zapper in a butcher's shop recorded from directly behind them. An environmental activist is gagged and bound. The crack of a jockey's whip on a horse in Dubai. The click and snap of ski boots into bindings. A donkey strains on nylon reins in the snow. Someone peeling off a wetsuit. The hiss of the heat tongs as they seal the end of the vas deferens tube in a vasectomy operation.

The football is still in the air; we hear it pass above our heads.

The squirt of hairspray. The squirt of air freshener. The squirt of red paint on a pine cone in a factory making Christmas decorations. The squirt of an asthma inhaler. The squirt of window cleaner. The squirt of One Direction-branded perfume. The squirt of antibacterial handwash in a law firm. The squirt of pepper spray into the face of a Black Lives Matter protester. The squirt of insulating foam from a can. The squirt of water onto a model's face on a suntan commercial shoot. The squirt of screenwash onto the windscreen of a tank in the midday heat. The squirt of a conditioner onto a dog's coat at Crufts. The squirt of a cheap deodorant onto a boy's armpit. The squirt of canned cheese onto a plate of nachos at a cinema in Malta. The squirt of vinegar onto chips. The squirt of a soda syphon in a BBC sound FX studio. The squirt of a small fire extinguisher in a toy factory. The squirt of butter-flavoured cooking spray onto a Teflon pan. The spray of an insect repellent on a neck. The squirt of shaving foam onto a crotch. The squirt of Roundup weedkiller on a driveway. The squirt of an athlete's-foot spray into a rugby boot. The squirt of lice treatment onto a chicken coop's wooden slats. The squirt of de-icer onto the bathroom window of a trailer. The squirt of a known carcinogen onto skin. The squirt of instant shoe polish. The squirt of sugar soap onto a bloodied, tiled floor. The squirt of suntan lotion into the eye of a young child. The squirt of lighter fuel onto a pile of A4 papers. The squirt of air fresheners again. The squirt of aerosol paint by a graffiti artist. The squirt of fake cream onto a stripper's nipples. Someone pukes vodka into a snowdrift in Vaasa.

The scratch of police dogs in the back of a van blend into the sound of a branch of an ancient oak tree through a council shredder on a residential street. The sound of a garden centre in a hurricane. Everyone giving birth right now. A child's toy bulldozer makes a piercing bleeping noise. More child's toys. It becomes an ocean of bleeps and whines and buzzes and fake chainsaw noises. It rises and rises. At its peak, now the rolling of a plastic wine cork for each bottle of wine made in France this year – 7.5 billion approximately – down the steps at the Sacré-Cœur. It is recorded from the bottom as they roll downwards towards the listener, towards fifty microphones set up. Someone has dug up many of the plastic things you threw away when you were a child and is firing them at your house from a series of cannons. An anti-aircraft gun spills empty shells onto concrete. A high-pass filter removes all the lower frequencies and then blends them until we just hear the tiny nervous rattling loops of silica gel packets found in the bottom of boxes of new TVs made today. The pouring of kitty litter into a plastic tray. The pouring of water from a kettle on an ants' nest. The sound Donald Trump's pen makes in a video as it skims across paper as he signs something. The glug of filthy cooking oil down a drain in the heat. A fox biting down on dyed food from a bin. A walnut cracked, a roadside bomb, a horse touching an electric fence, the slap of a cat flap, knitting machines, bread machines, mixing machines, sewing machines, machines for resetting the pins at bowling alleys, running machines, car-crushing machines, dog food.

A cat eats a bird on a porch while someone nearby reads an article about sound in the *New York Times*.

A group of hungry ramblers crunch over heather on a hilltop. A dog treads on a broken gin bottle on a beach. An empty cargo plane lands, we just hear a fragment: the exact moment the wheels hit the tarmac. There's a crackling and bubbling of brand new hot black asphalt settling just after it's been poured from the back of a paver. A can of Fanta shoved roughly in a rubbish bin on a train. A meagre morsel of tasteless, overcooked, chlorinated chicken stuffed in a mouth. Twelve concrete mixers turn and twelve builders bang the outsides with spades. The last strike is followed by the bang as a Jeep Cherokee hits a badger. Pause: a bee is against the inside of an office window again, trying to get to a flower it can see outside, but it's tired. A bear's stomach rumbles; we turn this sound up and up. The badger's corpse slumps down the metal grille of the car, a wet snort from its nostrils. A child rolls an upside-down snail down a metal slide in a play area. Two sisters in gloves pull a long continuous thread of carpet out of a poodle's backside after it has spent the last two days eating the fringes of it.

With a clicky noise and a spark, every pub and bar in London starts up their outside heaters. A whoosh followed by many small plops as the feeder for a salmon farm shoots food laced with pink dye out into the lake. A cutting of rosemary for supper. Someone dumps a broken microwave oven off a bridge into a canal with a splash. In Cuba a plastic basketball hits an abandoned fridge. A leisure sales regional manager is shaking a carton of unfinished rotten milk. A scraping, gouging of the bottom of an oil tanker against rough rocks in a storm, creating a gash, a hole. Reverb is added: it is an impulse response – a recording of the acoustic qualities of the inside of a giant Asda warehouse. A shoplifter runs off with a bottle of Pepsi.

We hear the amplified sound of a grasshopper as it lands on a just-varnished garden table and is suddenly stuck. Someone slips three corpses into a lake at dusk in quick succession.

A dry sound over the top: we hear people in Amsterdam pulling on the tear-strips of Amazon packages. The snap of elastic on a pair of blue plastic disposable overshoes. The tightening of cable ties.

Two chainsaws bang in the back of a brand new pickup truck as the owner drives too quickly over a tree root. Then slowly, some-one in the Hague opens a tin of Israeli olives. The stereo DPA mics are so close, and the sound slowed down so much, stretched until it feels like someone is peeling off the top of your head. Beneath it can just about be heard a forest on fire in Indonesia, fierce, crackling, rumbling. A girl carves the name of her lover in a eucalyptus tree in a city park in Melbourne. It's getting louder.

There's a smallish crowd at the game. The long, time-stretched, piercing squeal of a referee's whistle.

Maggots squeeze up beneath a worker's toes, going through the offcuts from Nile perch next to Lake Victoria. A coastguard's Land Rover drives over a starfish with a splitting noise. An owl strains against the short leather leash attached to a pole at a clifftop castle somewhere. A razor scrapes down a leg in a hotel bath. A gentoo penguin in an aquarium bumps its head on a wall depicting a mural of Antarctica. A daddy longlegs repeatedly bumps into a light bulb on a houseboat, but we just hear it for a few seconds. The dab of a blue paintbrush. A half-eaten polystyrene tub of prawns drops onto the leather seats of the pickup truck. A very light digital distortion is applied to all the sprinklers at Thanet Earth as they turn off; we hear the drip and ticking as everything settles down. Some sheep on Welsh hillsides are pissing in unison. The bubble of aquariums in a shop selling tropical fish. A plastic beer cup rolls down the harbour wall at Pelion in the wind towards the sea. A leak of something toxic into the water table, out of sight.

A sound designer and engineer have removed all the tin from several rivers in Germany and tied it all together in a row and are now dragging it behind several large trucks along the Avenue de L'indépendance in Yaoundé. A pig's tail is clipped off in a concrete shed with a metal roof. If you listen carefully, you can hear the clipping sound ping off the ceiling.

The click of magnets pulled together, switches making contact. The 14,000 chickens that are about to die in the next minute suddenly cluck quietly in unison. A butterfly flits in a corner against wallpaper in an ex-colonial administration building in Kenya. A filmmaker is making a short film of all the right-wing MPs in the UK mowing their lawns, but recorded from the nearest public road, heard through the open window of the editor's room. Someone is spraying fake blood onto a mattress. There's a huge can of rapeseed oil knocked over and it's glugging its contents everywhere.

Someone runs their hands up a rusted flagpole and listens to the paint flaking off. A slug makes its way vertically up the outside of a greenhouse; there's a contact mic on the other side of the glass to record it. Schoolgirls aged between five and six are sharpening their pencils slowly, as quietly as possible, while we listen to the slug's slow journey.

A nest full of new chicks in a hedge at a literary festival strain to be heard over the campers at dawn, and squawk increasingly loudly up to the sky. Twenty to thirty dogs tied up outside supermarkets want their owners back.

A depleted uranium shell grinds unheard beneath a rock as a taxi drives over it in Iraq. A lorry reverses up to the loading bay of a flower distribution warehouse in Savannah. The milking machine on a cow strains and pulls. A truck carrying pigs to market has overturned, spilling now-dead animals across the highway. We hear the shovel of a single person trying to clean up the carnage. Another person is digging for lugworms on a beach. The buzzing of Barcelona city lights is amplified and spread wide across the image. The flap of the wings of a moth above the pitch in a packed football stadium. The hum of Edinburgh from Calton Hill.

A bluebottle is flying around in a theatre during a show. A sheep is shorn of its fleece but we are recording it from a kestrel-shaped kite flown at some distance above. A box of apricots with moths in shifts backwards on a forklift truck. A dog is on the back of a bicycle on its way to being neutered. A barnacle ground off the side of a boat. A rough-legged buzzard is pecking at a radio transmitter attached to its leg. In the same rhythm, a family is crunching through leaves on the way to a firework show. The crack of lobster shells in brasseries. A huge carp is straining on a line, spinning the reel. A bat flies into a catch net.

A string bag full of footballs drops out of an estate car. An industrial vat of glue, bubbling. The peeling-back of the plastic layer on a ready-meal curry.

An artist has made a work in which they have bought the same types and number of animals about to be killed for food tonight in Washington and instead is walking them in a line from a restaurant in Paris to a special golden incinerator located in a field outside Monaco. A musician has asked forty-eight people to stamp on a snail shell made out of pastry for an album about Brexit. A scientist has assembled sixty people on a boat and asked them to blow across the tops of hollow animal bones she has excavated from different Neolithic sites across Europe.

The daughter reaches up and squeezes her father's hip as he peers towards the sun, looking for the ball.

Someone is watching the movie of *The Woman in the Dunes* in the back of a tour bus and we hear the sound of sand under the actors' feet on the screen. A haul of dead sharks is tipped overboard a trawling vessel, but it is recorded from fifty metres down. The whirring of the big data servers storing the words of this book somewhere in California heard from the location where employees are supposed to meet in the event of a fire, but where now a cleaner, learning German on headphones, is unwrapping a new packet of cigarettes and gulping vitamin water. A tap from a standpipe is running dry and the bucket placed beneath it to catch the drips has fallen over.

All the kids' jungle-themed noisy toys with battery life left in them recorded deep in the world's landfill sites. They make the occasional warped monkey or lion noise as the pressure changes. While we listen to that, two students are peeling the plastic wrappers off stolen CDs right now. A stream of water hosing down an ambulance. A maths teacher has diarrhoea. A limousine driver in Bolivia emptying his ashtray into a puddle in a quiet car park.

Fishermen sitting by a lake not far from Niigata, Japan are slowly reeling in. A Caterpillar digger has been slowly approaching from some distance. It has been sitting underneath all the other sounds since the chickens went silent, and is now coming to the foreground of the stereo image. We hear it moving over uneven ground, closer, louder and then a miserable grind and churn as it pushes over an ancient olive tree. A picture editor is photoshopping nipples out of a make-up advert. A celebrity chef is sniffing a lemon. Suddenly – bang, a seagull into a jet engine. A stabbing of the 500 million straws to be used today into McDonald's cups. They squeak as they rub against the plastic of the lid. Someone sits down too hard on a crate of Moroccan oranges in the back of a lorry. A small mountain of pea gravel is dumped in a hole. A brown bear stands on a frozen river. It creaks a little beneath her. A fishmonger bursts the swim bladder of a whiting with a pop. A van and trailer full of white sugar overturns by a roundabout near a river. At Lake Coniston, teenagers are skimming stones. A bag of ice cubes now dropped in a child's seat on the back of a bike to be ridden back to a party. A group of volunteers combs a stony beach for clues to a murder. A hiker in the Alps trips over the sole of an old walking boot on the path. The hiss of a gas leak. The slow tearing of a sachet that holds a tea bag. Different car number plates are hit by 73,984 insects at once. Then a different collection of 73,984 insects come towards the listener from all directions. Crack – a lightning strike on a Hindu temple. A flock of starlings startled by a gunshot. Garden chairs off a ship's balcony in high seas. A huge drill strikes oil with a bang, gush, spurt – a microphone has been mounted right in the thickest part of the liquid. An overwhelming waterfall of Garnier Fructis shampoo. Farmers swinging by their necks from ropes. Every plant dug up since this chapter started, heaped in a pile. Chewing gum sticking to the sole of a nurse's sneaker on the Marshall Islands. A mouse with its paws in a plastic tray of poison, unwittingly pushing it against the floor to make a scraping noise. A DIY shelf going up. Half-finished KFC bags thrown out of slammed VW Golfs. A camper spits toothpaste into the bush. An oil executive and lobbyist sign a contract over negronis. Plastic bags flap furiously in strong wind in trees. A crampon hits rock. A small canister of nitrous oxide dropped in a bathroom sink at a party. A factory. A factory. A war. A war. A climber is drilling into a cliff to insert something to hold his rope. The shattered glass of a cider bottle as it hits a dry river bed. A knife stabbed through a kidney. Someone biting into a grape that has too much pesticide residue on it. A rare beetle crossing a road crushed by a motorbike. A plant leaf snipped in a lab. Someone trimming a bush into the shape of a whale. Fifty-three boxes of Prozac shaking, trembling. A lunch break at a factory that makes cheap plastic toys for the covers of children's magazines. Jet skis recorded from just under the surface of the water. A kid puking over the side of a wheelbarrow. A trained otter in Pakistan dives for fish. The champagne tipping over the cap of a winning racing driver. The grind of sand in an oily cog. The foundations of a new dam going in. Light bulbs pop. A cricket ball through the skylight of an art gallery. An insurance salesman stands on a baby turtle by accident. Grains firing through the metal tubes of a combine harvester, recorded from inside. A disposable barbeque dropped into the sea with a splash and a hiss.

A Harley-Davidson drives at speed past the football pitch. The ball is still in the air. A tree shivers.

On concrete by the Humber Bank Wall, a fisherman is pulling the skin off a Dover sole, peeling it back in a single, simple gesture as the skin is torn from the flesh. A camera crew is filming it. The producer steps back, startled by the incoming swoop of a herring gull, loses their footing and topples backwards over the wall and into the water. As we hear the splash, a bee pushes its sting into an ear. This is loud now. A mosquito lands on sleeping flesh. The sound is unnaturally high. The snap of a crocodile's jaw onto a head. The pecking of a hooked beak on a ribcage. The crackle of a fire spreading through eaves. Brutal rain on temporary plastic roofs. Frozen water creaking sharply underneath a line of men in boots. The amputation of a leg. The crisping of flesh under intense heat. The thwack of a tree branch on a power line. A lightning strike in reply. We're accelerating now. The rapid digging of a mole beneath a neoclassical statue. The tapping of woodworm. The scrabble of wasps in the plasterwork by beams of an old farmhouse. The sound of a bridge shifting and cracking. All the pens, paper and stationery in the offices of a car manufacturer shaking during an earthquake. The scalding of boiling water on skin. A brief sound of the collapse and crumble of lava down the side of a volcano. A cascade of bird shit. The yank of a typhoon ripping a roof off. The pelt of hailstones against wooden boards. The splash of thick black oil down a trouser leg. The cracking of an antler through a pelvis. The scrape of a rake across the concrete floor of an industrial duck shed. An elongation now, an excerpt of the time-lapse sound of an ivy bush growing around a shopping trolley sped up by a factor of one hundred and played at Café OTO as the opening act. The sound of mould growing inside a fridge. Acid rain falling. Toxic fog on an in-breath. Sand in your ears. Snow and salt and slush crashing through a hotel window. If bacteria makes a noise, it's heard here, amplified, distorted. Ice spreading rapidly across a slip road. A wild boar loose on a cricket pitch. Waves hitting a living-room window. The stamp of an elephant on a car bonnet. A house dropping off the edge of an eroding cliff. The scuttle of a scorpion across the floor of a holiday apartment. A rat's tail slipping through dust beneath a sink you once stood at. A spider leaps down at the microphone from a hidden web. A pit bull bites through a foot. A rusty nail in a knee. A frostbitten toe coming away from the foot. A glutinous splintering and cracking of sodden timber at the same time as we hear a large whoosh as doors give way in homes and floodwater rushes in. A tornado slices through a town. A snake hisses as it appears from the side of a fake log. A nettle plant stings as it is picked, amplified. A splinter of rusty metal from a farmer's gate pierces a hand. A huge chunk of snow and ice calves away from an iceberg. A river bursts its banks. A flame licks around straw. A sharp splinter into a heel. The multiplication of an incurable cancer. A worm slips unheard through your gut. A heart skips, stutters. The rustle of branched thorns as an embossed golf ball disappears into thick bushes.

The deflated football hits a tree, drops to the ground and comes to a rest, the branches settle themselves. The daughter runs towards it, picks it up and heads across the pitch towards the highway.

A forest is listening out for you, waiting to hear you coming.

5.

Largo

To stop

An in-breath

    of someone you love
    towards the end
    of their life

    Followed by the
    silence
    before you jump into a cold lake

    Then an out-breath

    of that
    person
    you love

    Then the silence
    before a jury
    announces their verdict

Then an in-breath

    Then the silence
    of a baby just before it starts breathing again
    after a seemingly endless pause

    An out-breath

    The silence
    of a painter just before
    the brush touches the paper

An in-breath

The silence
before
a long-desired kiss

An out-breath

The silence
before
the vicar says amen

An in-breath

The silence
just before a kettle starts heating up after
the switch has been flicked on

An out-breath

The silence
just before the needle of a syringe
breaks the skin

An in-breath

The silence
inside a large plane on a runway before
taking off on a night flight

An out-breath

The silence
before a prayer at
a family dinner

An in-breath

The silence
before the light
turns green

An out-breath

The silent lull
during a long, violent argument
before
the other person says something

An in-breath

The silence
of a TV presenter alone in a dressing room
focusing themselves before walking out to present a live show

An out-breath

The silence
at the end of an opera before
a standing ovation

An in-breath

The silence
just before a firework
explodes

An out-breath

The silence
before a surgeon makes a
cut into flesh

An in-breath

The silence
on an old DVD recording before
Simon Cowell says yes

An out-breath

The silence
in a troop carrier on its way
towards a battle

An in-breath

The silence
of a golf ball after it lands
in a bunker

An out-breath

The silence
just before a group of strangers
face death together

An in-breath

The silence
in a divorce court before
the judge enters

An out-breath

The silence
before you decide to buy something
you know you can't afford

An in-breath

The silence
before you realise you're going
too fast

An out-breath

The silence
of a lobster with elastic bands
on its claws

An in-breath

The mid-afternoon silence
in a home for
the elderly

An out-breath

The silence
of the doctor as she checks something
in your notes

An in-breath

The silence
of an
absent parent

An out-breath

The silence
of a
child's playground at night

An in-breath

The silence
when you realise your body has
changed shape

An out-breath

The silence
of a
pile of dirty clothes

An in-breath

The silence
before
relief and rescue arrives

An out-breath

The silence
in between pressing 'play' and
the start of your favourite piece of music

An in-breath

The silence
between the bleeps on a smoke alarm that indicate
the battery is running out

An out-breath

The silence
as you wait for night
to end

An in-breath

A moment of silence
inside a losing football crowd towards the end of a match
when nobody is singing

An out-breath

The silence
as an actor
forgets their lines

An in-breath

The silence
after all the heating
turns off at night

An out-breath

Then the silence
of a corrupt official as he looks at
your documents

An in-breath

The silence
on shutdown just after a computer fan has stopped whirring
but before the screen goes black

An out-breath

The silence
in the back of a sealed shipping container
at a border

An in-breath

The silence
of the person checking you in to a motel at 4.45 a.m.
as they deliberately stare at their monitor screen instead of you

An out-breath

The silence
during
non-consensual sex

An in-breath

The silence
between the coughs during the gap between the movements
of a performance of a Mahler symphony

An out-breath

The silence
inside a headmaster's office
while you wait outside

An in-breath

The silence
of a ketchup bottle
at a roadside food van

An out-breath

The silence
between a teenager asking someone out
on a date for the first time and that person saying no

An in-breath

The silence
when your phone has run out of battery
in a critical situation

An out-breath

The silence
inside
a lift full of strangers

An in-breath

The silence
of a small antique black metal box
whose lid won't open

An out-breath

The silence
when a man in uniform enters
your train compartment

An in-breath

The silence
of an elderly woman in front of a van Gogh painting
at the Musée d'Orsay

An out-breath

The silence
of two people as they look up at the
enormity of the night sky

An in-breath

The silence
following a knock on the door by
housekeeping in a hotel

An out-breath

The silence
on the other end of the line
while the person tries to process your paperwork

An in-breath

The silence
of a dog at your feet,
looking up

An out-breath

The silence
of a washing machine as it waits to decide
when to let you open the door

An in-breath

The silence
of a child about to be sick
in the back of a car

An out-breath

The silence
inside your house
as a policeman walks down your driveway

An in-breath

The silence
of someone standing still and looking in a fridge
trying to work out if there's something to eat

An out-breath

The silence
of watching an act of horror unfold
in real time

An in-breath

The silence
of a cave painting
in the Ardèche

An out-breath

The silence
of a shadow by a
street lamp

An in-breath

The silence
on a bus when you suddenly realise everyone else has got off,
the engine has been switched off
and the bus isn't going
any further

An out-breath

The silence
inside every empty fake present box under
the Hamley's Christmas tree

An in-breath

The silence
of
a flat tyre

An out-breath

The silence
between
bombs falling

An in-breath

The silence
of someone standing reading a letter by the front door
but still wearing their outdoor coat

An out-breath

The silence
when you realise you're about to see a new naked body
for the first time

An in-breath

The silence
of a window
too small to climb through

An out-breath

The silence
of staring at a new coat in a mirror
as you try to get a better understanding of how you look

An in-breath

The silence
of a small Mediterranean hilltop town
in the heat of a Sunday afternoon

An out-breath

The silence
of a trans kid in the
bathroom

An in-breath

The silence
of a skeleton in a
science laboratory

An out-breath

The silence
after you turn the key in the door of a
new house

An in-breath

The silence
on a night bus full of cleaners
going to work

An out-breath

The silence
of a partner on the phone
to a parent

An in-breath

The silence
while you wait for an urgent, important file to upload
but it's going too slowly, has even stopped

An out-breath

The silence
in a shop as you wait to be told of the price of an
unmarked item of jewellery you suspect is particularly expensive

An in-breath

The silence
of watching someone else
trying to make a decision

An out-breath

The silence
of a person who never
came home

An in-breath

The silence
of a
dried-up lake

An out-breath

The silence
in a hot-air balloon
after the gas has been fired

An in-breath

The silence
between
raindrops dripping off a gutter

An out-breath

The silence
while someone decides whether to buy stolen goods
or not

An in-breath

The silence
of someone reading
these words

An out-breath

The silence
inside a sandwich inside a fridge inside a shop
inside a station

An in-breath

The silence
as you try and comprehend
the numbers of people drowned

An out-breath

The silence
of a candidate waiting to learn about
an election result

An in-breath

The silence
in the empty toilets
during a presentation at an arms fair

An out-breath

The silence
of a
passport queue

An in-breath

The silence
of offices in a glass skyscraper,
seen from the outside

An out-breath

The silence
of a shop
with nothing on the shelves

An in-breath

The silence
of an apple core
next to a child's car seat

An out-breath

The silence
in the empty cloakroom of a museum
where all the bags are kept during the day

An in-breath

The silence
of a man's hand
resting on a woman's leg

An out-breath

The silence
of pedestrians
when a hearse goes past

An in-breath

The silence
of a favourite pair of shoes
by the front door

An out-breath

The silence
of a child's bedroom at night
when the child isn't there

An in-breath

The silence
of an audience at a Radiohead gig in Japan
between songs

An out-breath

The silence
of someone else's possessions handed to you
in a see-through plastic bag

An in-breath

The silence
of a broken water fountain
in an abandoned town square in the heat

An out-breath

The silence
of the Queen's
vintage wine collection

An in-breath

The silence
of
Rekia Boyd

An out-breath

The silence
of an unread book
about gardening

An in-breath

The silence
of
a prayer

An out-breath

The silence
of
an impenetrable wall

An in-breath

The silence
of a group of people as they sit and listen to someone
speaking, reading aloud

An out-breath

The silence
of exhausted workers
at the end of a long shift

An in-breath

The silence
of empty second homes
at Christmas time

An out-breath

The silence
of a stone picked up near a mountain
and taken home

An in-breath

The silence
of a beetle
set in resin

An out-breath

The silence
of a Kyoto temple
while the hot tea in front of you cools down

An in-breath

The silence
in a nail bar as someone paints the nails of
the final customer of the day

An out-breath

The silence
when you realise
you are in danger

An in-breath

The silence
of an empty, closed motorway
two miles after a serious accident

An out-breath

The silence
as orchestral percussionists
count their rests

An in-breath

The silence
of a soldier
overseas

An out-breath

The silence
inside a border and customs
waiting room

An in-breath

The silence
of a nearly built
bridge

An out-breath

The silence
of a potter surveying a newly finished earthenware bowl
after the wheel has stopped

An in-breath

The silence
of one glove on a
park bench

An out-breath

The silence
between someone asking someone to marry them
and the answer

An in-breath

The silence
while someone younger than you
checks your ID

An out-breath

The silence
of a first night
in prison

An in-breath

The silence
when you don't know what to say or write or do or how to get
out of bed

An out-breath

The silence
at the end of a cup
of tea

An in-breath

The silence
inside
a just-finished coffin

An out-breath

The silence
of a nest of eggs
with no birds present

An in-breath

The silence
of ice
between creaks and splinters

An out-breath

The silence
in the back of a taxi when you think
you're deliberately being taken the wrong way

An in-breath

The silence
in the middle of a calm sea in
the summertime

An out-breath

The silence
as a shop's card reader
dials your bank to see if there is
enough money in your account
when you know there
possibly isn't

An in-breath

The silence
of a flower arrangement
tied to a lamp post

An out-breath

The silence
as heard from a hiding place,
working out if the other person
has passed the door and
carried on walking,
or stopped

An in-breath

The silence
inside an air pocket
at the bottom of a collapsed building

An out-breath

The silence
when you realise
someone doesn't believe you

An in-breath

The silence
of an armed guard as he decides
whether to let you in or not

An out-breath

The silence
as a table of diners waits for the last person
to give their order to a busy waitress

An in-breath

The silence
of a human-rights lawyer
in the boot of a car

An out-breath

The silence
by a new grave
with no headstone yet

An in-breath

The silence
of a large pile of unopened mail
in the dark

An out-breath

The silence
as you wait to see if the person upstairs
is asleep yet

An in-breath

A minute of
silent
remembrance

An out-breath

The silence
of meeting someone again
as they try to remember your name

An in-breath

The silence
of a government
when another nation is in need

An out-breath

The silence
of someone near you
looking at something on their phone

An in-breath

The silence
of a pig's heart in a jar of formaldehyde
on a shelf

An out-breath

The silence
of a barber shop when an army general
walks in and sits down

An in-breath

The silence
of
a landscape from space

An out-breath

The silence
of
a record collection

An in-breath

The silence
as you wait to see if a complicated Wi-Fi password
has been accepted by the network

An out-breath

The silence
after a distraught phone call from a family member
is suddenly cut off

An in-breath

The silence
of four nervous young men
in a first-class railway carriage

An out-breath

The silence
of a row of new tractors
by a factory

An in-breath

The silence
of children's shoes
that are now too small

An out-breath

The silence
of someone hiding underneath
a just-dead person

An in-breath

The silence
of
an empty wallet

An out-breath

The silence
of
no food

An in-breath

The silence
of
a felled ash tree

An out-breath

The silence
in between
blows

An in-breath

The silence
of an unopened jar of honey
at the bottom of a bag

An out-breath

The silence
of all the cars lined up in a car-rental place
waiting to be picked

An in-breath

The silence
of a wooden yellow pencil
with a snapped tip

An out-breath

The silence
between a lightning strike and
the wait for thunder

An in-breath

The silence
of
an empty dance floor

An out-breath

The silence
as someone looks really closely
at you

An in-breath

The silence
between gags
as someone vomits nearby

An out-breath

The silence
of an unseen politician
in the back of a passing car

An in-breath

The silence
of
used confetti on the floor

An out-breath

The silence
of
a child on an iPad

An in-breath

The silence
of
a broken heater

An out-breath

> The silence
> while looking for a light ahead somewhere.
> Through the dark

> An in-breath

> The silence
> of
> a locked gate

An out-breath

> The silence
> of
> an unreported injustice

> An in-breath

> The silence
> of a school at night
> in winter

An out-breath

> The silence
> of an expensive dress in a window,
> seen from the outside

> An in-breath

> The silence
> of
> a taxidermy owl

An out-breath

The silence
when you realise
you're dying

An in-breath

The silence
of
Paul Dacre's bookshelf

An out-breath

The silence
of an envelope of
test results

An in-breath

The silence
between
strings on a squash racket

An out-breath

The silence
of an expensive but unplayed piano
in a living room on the twenty-eighth floor

An in-breath

The silence
while people listen to an announcement telling them why
the train is delayed

An out-breath

The silence
of
the Crown Jewels

An in-breath

The silence
of
a pack of supermarket mushrooms

An out-breath

The silence
of
Fred Astaire's shoe lasts

An in-breath

The short sudden silence
on a very rainy motorway as you briefly drive under a bridge
and for tiny moment there is no rain on the roof

An out-breath

The silence
of
a missing limb

An in-breath

The silence
of
a dead plant

An out-breath

An empty
bombed-out
building

An in-breath

The silence
when you realise you're lost
in the snow

An out-breath

The silence
where a mosque
used to be

An in-breath

The silence
after an email you sent remains unreplied to
several weeks later

An out-breath

The silence
in a woodland having just thought you heard a woodpecker
and waiting for it to start making the drilling noise again

An in-breath

The silence
after
you've just told a lie

An out-breath

The silence
of a dead body in the
cellar below

An in-breath

The silence
during bad turbulence on a plane
over the North Sea

An out-breath

The silence
straight after a loud noise downstairs
in a house at night,
but you're on your own

An in-breath

The silence
of a young girl
applying mascara

An out-breath

The silence
after an unpleasant heckle on someone's
first stand-up comedy gig

An in-breath

The silence
in a small vintage clothes shop
after the music playing from the speakers runs out

An out-breath

The silence
of an unlit fire
in the grate

An in-breath

The silence
in a bathroom just after someone goes in
and locks the door

An out-breath

The silence
after the test drive of a new car
while the salesperson waits to see if you like it or not

An in-breath

The silence
after an unrequited
'good morning'

An out-breath

The silence
after a crucial but tiny screw of something you are building or
repairing has fallen on the floor and stops rolling,
settling somewhere out of sight

An in-breath

The silence
after a zip gets stuck on an overpacked bag and refuses
to go forwards or backwards

An out-breath

> The silence
> after
> a racist joke

An in-breath

> The silence
> after
> a bird flies into a window

An out-breath

> The silence
> at the end of a presentation when the moderator
> asks the audience, 'Any questions?'

An in-breath

> The silence
> after a waiter puts down an expensive but tiny portion
> of unimpressive vegetables

An out-breath

> The silence
> after you realise
> you just killed someone

An in-breath

> The silence
> after young children
> have gone to bed

An out-breath

The silence
after you work out you are in totally
the wrong place

An in-breath

The silence
after you remembered you left your passport on the table
of the last place you stayed at

An out-breath

The silence
after someone tells you
they are leaving you

An in-breath

The silence
when you've entered the incorrect password
for the last time

An out-breath

The silence
of a tap
when water no longer comes out

An in-breath

The silence
after having just pressed the door buzzer at
a job interview

An out-breath

The silence
after the pin's been pulled out of
a grenade

An in-breath

The silence
at the end of a play
about domestic violence

An out-breath

The silence
just after the electric meter
runs out of money

An in-breath

The silence
after opening an unwanted gift
in the presence of the giver

An out-breath

The silence
of an empty backstage
after a big concert

An in-breath

The silence
after someone has tried the wrong key
in a front door

An out-breath

The silence
after you've asked a friend
for a lot of money

An in-breath

The silence
after the curtains are closed by a stranger
in the same room as you

An out-breath

The silence
after you realise you can't
remember

An in-breath

The silence
after someone is thrown out
of an aeroplane

An out-breath

The silence
after a new mall
is completed

An in-breath

The silence
after saying goodbye
at a station

An out-breath

The silence
after you realise nobody has called
to see how you are

An in-breath

The silence
in a house after everyone else
has gone to work

An out-breath

The silence
after a mercenary
has put a hood over your head

An in-breath

The silence
after someone tells you something you never realised they felt,
a secret

An out-breath

The silence
after you send undercooked food
back to the kitchen

An in-breath

The silence
after the safety catch
has been released from a gun

An out-breath

The silence
after lying back
in the bath

An in-breath

The silence
of concrete where there
used to be grass

An out-breath

The silence
after
you run out of fuel

An in-breath

The silence
after the last member of a family dies,
leaving no children or relatives

An out-breath

The silence
after an artist shows a curator
their terrible new work

An in-breath

The silence
after
a birthday party

An out-breath

The silence
between parents on a hike,
who have run out of water

An in-breath

The silence
after someone unknown
closes the front door

An out-breath

The silence
after an alarm has
stopped

An in-breath

The silence
as people start to get dressed at the end
of a swingers party

An out-breath

The silence
when a phone stops ringing after
two to three minutes

An in-breath

The silence
after a whip has met
flesh

An out-breath

The lengthening silence
between
the beats of a failing heart

An in-breath

The silence
of a loved one
through glass

An out-breath

The silence
after a radio has been
turned off

A shuddering breath

The silence
of a pond just after a
frog jumps in

A broken breath

The silence
just before a wine bottle
lets go of its cork

A curtailed, muffled breath

The silence
after a bee has left
a flower

6

Grave

To love

There's a low buzzing made up of several noises. There is a 50 Hz cycle, an earth hum. Layered on top of that there is the vibration from a fan, which is also creating a hum, but this is just the vibration of the fan motor, as it's mounted against an inner metal frame that's hidden from view but vibrates in sympathy, but out of time, with the rest of the structure. The motor driving the fan has a slight whine. There is also the movement of the air itself from the fan, a stable but uneven noise. The thin blades on the fan are oscillating as they spin so there are minor variations. It feels like a wave.

It is part of the sound of a freezer lodged in a corner on an uneven floor surface and is shuddering in tiny movements. We can hear this if we get right down on our hands and knees and pay close attention. As a consequence, a small area of the whole structure is rubbing a little against the wall, bumping very slightly onto a tiled wall. Some tiles, though, are recently broken and one has a sharp edge. Every fifteen seconds or so the freezer rocks a little further than usual and catches the sharp edge of one of these tiles. It adds an occasional tiny spike in the sound in the mid range, a dry, short click. You wouldn't necessarily know it was from a tile if heard in isolation. For the most part, these are minute sounds that barely register.

There's an occasional gust of wind that blows a little dust onto the foot near the front of the appliance. The cheapish metal footing rings a little metallically as the dust hits it. A tiny sound, but there nonetheless.

A jerky scratch, followed by an excessively long pause is possibly a mouse, out of sight. The gaps are long enough to make you think that you imagined it.

There is a need to think sensitively about how to mic this up, as it isn't appropriate, due to the nature of the scene, to rig the whole place with microphones. On the other hand, someone needs to hear and record this sound for ever.

We live in this collection of sounds for a while: the familiar hum of a freezer, a light gust of early evening wind blowing some loose sand. And a breath.

The breath itself is uneven. At times it has a pattern, but every few breaths there is a heaviness in the out-breath, the mouth closed. We can catch the air coming down a single nostril. It has the shape of a mini sigh, a fast crescendo to a sudden stop. This keeps happening; the shape of the sound is the same each time. After a minute or so, we hear a long juddering breath in, as if the owner of the lungs hasn't managed to get enough oxygen during the preceding minutes. When the breath is bigger either in or out, there is a slight movement in the clothes. The polyester in the jumper rubs a little against itself around the arms, the fibres bristling unevenly against each other. A plastic-soled sandal twists a little bit in the dust. At the same time, a tiny rock trapped beneath the sole, but still bigger than the dust and sand, grinds slightly against itself as the sandal turns. And when it stops it feels like silence again. But it's not silent; we can still hear the motor of the fan, the blades spinning.

There are other noises. There is a small overhead fluorescent light causing a familiar dreary buzz that would only really become apparent if we turned it off. Still we hear the breath.

There is also a ticking we can just about hear, although for some reason it seems to come and go. A watch, maybe. If we wanted to, we could hear their heartbeat buried somewhere beneath the clothing.

The dullest of sounds, this time a hand placed carefully on the left shoulder. In the background there is another buzzing, humming. It feels like it gets closer then moves away again. It's a very uneven sound and it would be hard to point to where it was coming from if you were actually there. It, too, has a combination of hums, whines – all mechanical noises. It might be a drone, it might be a lawnmower being used on a small patch of grass or it may be some kind of power tool. It seems to be ignoring where we are, though, choosing to wander. It is a viscous, unrelenting noise, but its journey is meandering, unclear. It is not so loud as to disturb the stillness of the scene, but it feels like it is always audible. On the extreme right of the stereo image there is another mechanical drone, hum. This time from a generator that chugs away unsteadily in the distance. Again it is very quiet, but it is present. It may be that during the recording of this scene, the generator runs out of fuel, in which case we immediately notice its absence, even if we hadn't noticed its presence before.

A very distant ambulance siren briefly comes in on the same note as one of the smaller fans spinning on the freezer. The drone/mower/tool dips a little and for a split second they are in unison before each sound continues in its own direction, the tempo, rhythm and key differing wildly now as they stick rigidly to their own part.

A moped burns past, its tiny, holed exhaust spurting a violent tear through the sound field, moving from right to left in the image. Since we are on a relatively steep hill, the sound, if recorded properly, should feel as if it not only moves from right to left but from lower down to further up the slope. The squealing buzz of it creates waves of sound that slosh about, fluid and angular between the different buildings.

At a strain we could potentially hear a radio, or perhaps a TV. We couldn't distinguish whether it was even words or music but on repeat listens, we would spot it as part of the soundscape. There are no schoolchildren playing, nor the sound of water fountains.

A pigeon call. Unanswered.

A cup of some sort, filled. A hesitant pair of footsteps that stop some way short of where we are.

The very distant rattle of gunfire in two short bursts. Then nothing.

A whisper nearby. A subtle rearranging of the balance of feet.

The slim slide and shift of paper.

The twist of a fan.

A clicking noise. It has a constant, nervous rhythm to it, but it runs and stops in uneven measures. The intensity and volume remains about the same. If you were to look at a technical analysis of the sound, it would have a low rumble that was almost inaudible on the file but it would have sharp peaks further up the audio spectrum where this clicking was. What the microphone picks up, though, isn't necessarily the truth and, in fact, it is more of a flicking sound in real life. Someone is resting a finger inside a weirdly dipped, curled plastic protrusion made from a colourful sticker that, as well as having faded, has also lost some of its glue and is starting to peel off on one corner. It has created a curl that is a perfect fit for a finger. The sticker is for an Al-Aroussa lemon-flavoured ice cream, and it is one of many attached to the front panel of the freezer. The thickness of the plastic of the sticker, thicker than a sticker you'd find in a house, has meant that the curl itself is a particularly tight one, creating tension and resistance for the finger. The net result is a crisp click and a subsequent plucking motion from the finger. The finger itself has no rings and the nails are short. It has a thickness to it and as well as having patches of both wetness and dust, there is something unfamiliar under the end of the nail. The fingers on other hand are pressed to the skin of the skull, the hand supporting the head. The fingers occasionally slip a small distance, disturbing the thickness of the hair for a fraction of a second. The elbow is resting on the arm of a simple plastic chair. While each of the chair's legs are the same length, the unevenness of the ground has meant that the chair isn't flat on the floor and the chair is also occasionally rocking, but only slightly. Each sparse rocking of the chair sends a little stab of gravity up the leg and where the metal of the leg meets the plastic of the chair, there is a bump in the lower frequencies and a nearly inaudible version of a snap.

From the sounds so far we can work out that this is a man.

The creak of knuckles as a hand grips something made of cotton and nylon too hard. It has a pair of plastic eyes, one slightly more worn than the other, and small plastic toes that pop out from fur. There is a metal stud near one of the belt loops on his jeans that one of the toes catches on once during the five-minute recording.

Still the occasional tick of a hot-water urn or metallic kettle.

A mosquito appears for a while, coming in and out of focus. And then stops.

The artificial sound of a camera shutter: someone taking a photo on a phone.

We notice the breath again. Uneven, occasionally shuddering. A resettling on the chair. The hum of the freezer, the droning, the wind, the dust, the presence of a few other people in silence.

An imperceptible noise – the sound of an ache, an unbearable pain. Organs moving fluids around more slowly than usual. New types of chemicals pulsing through arteries. Neurons firing unheard in the brain, signals passing up and down a spinal cord. A skeleton barely moving but whose tiny movements are measured and recorded as the bones shift. Feet resting in preparation for the long walk to come. Tiny hair follicles on the arms laying low. The fingernails have temporarily paused their growth, but the keratin layers still rub against each other in sympathy. Wax is settling inside the ears. Sweat is forming but not yet ready to reveal itself. Saliva is absorbing itself into the lining of the mouth. Kidneys are still washing toxins from the blood. The cartilage between elbows that helped to grip is already stiffening, albeit temporarily. Lactic acid is forming. Cells are replicating, folding.

A stomach in no rush for food.

An uneven sense of air.

The sound of skin forming into furrows.

The finger stops picking at the sticker briefly. The generator seems to be running, but the weird drone noise has gone. Everyone is still, waiting. The bird takes off from a fence. Inside the freezer, if we took the time to listen carefully, we'd hear the sound of ice crystals forming inside the body of a child.

7.

Tenuto

To be rich

In London, the head of a sticky mop, twisted, turning, squeezed into a plastic bucket. The remnants of blood, water dripping in uneven thick droplets. The shuffle of a nylon tunic, and the slip of a pair of bangles down a wrist as a hand moves further along the mop handle. Another twist of the mop, fewer drops. An unexpected cough. A security turnstile. Someone else is pulling on gloves as a supervisor repeatedly flips their phone in silence.

Elsewhere, inside the cheap plastic toy model of a refuse truck that was received as a present some years ago, a two-year-old battery has leaked and created a kind of crusty webbing between the toy's driver's seat and the door. This acidic crust has created a tiny, subtle high-end rub at the point of impact that otherwise would have been a simple, smooth, brittle snap when stood upon by an oblivious parent. As we hear that noise, the stereo image opens up to a stacked soundscape of two communities of families living on and among rubbish dumps somewhere in the world, each recorded from an omni microphone slung from an extra-long series of cables strung beneath a pair of cranes.

Bulldozers, seagulls, a multitude of drowned-out voices. Grinding, cracking, torn plastic, mushy paper, rotten food and metal. Glass shards and broken wood. It gets louder.

Two broken fake-gold chairs fall from a truck near a severed limb or hand from medical waste, lying on top of a rubbish pile. One bird defecates onto the screen of an old, dead TV facing upwards to the sky, another one defecates onto an abandoned shopping basket. A glob of phlegm from a passenger on a motorbike in Cambodia onto a street sign saying 'Two-way road'. A pair of soiled, once-white, now-grey underpants hits the bottom of a plastic bin in an old people's home. Someone is wading through a blocked sewer. Clumps of dirt fall off bright pink wellington boots near a neon-lit puddle. A demolition ball smashes through a tower block. A chimney sweep forces a brush up a flue. The shovel of spades as women separate ore from sand in a coltan mine in Fungamwaka. A mechanic drops a used oil filter on the floor of a garage. A dead mouse slips further behind a cooker. A red-topped black plastic wheelie bin blown over in the wind with a bang in an alleyway. Piles of rotten leaves are pulled in handfuls from a pipe. Under a sink, a white plastic U-bend fixture comes undone with two violent slops, spilling its contents of congealed hair, blood and spit on a bathroom floor. A small bag full of dog turds swung hastily into a bramble patch in a forest. Someone stamps on a sealed bag of out-of-date and now rotten spinach. Bruised and unwashed toenails being clipped in a caravan. Dust is shaken from plastic plants. A mouldy tea towel that's been used to mop up spilt milk and then left for two weeks is dropped in a Waitrose carrier bag by someone with a green paper mask over their mouth and rubber gloves. A lit cigarette is flicked into two centimetres of last night's red wine in the bottom of a stained mug with a spitting sound. An eagle ripping a sinew from a decaying bone. Somewhere humid, an elderly woman stands on a bent paperclip, which punctures the sole of her flip-flop. A flame cracks a glass pipe. A pair of chipped toy marbles hits a corrugated-iron roof with a short popping bang and then roll down the remaining length before falling off the end, one onto a tarpaulin and one into an empty plastic bucket.

Bulldozers, seagulls, a multitude of drowned-out voices. Grinding, cracking, torn plastic, mushy paper, rotten food and metal. Glass shards and broken wood. It gets louder.

An R2-D2 Star Wars alarm clock going off in the bottom of a metal dustbin. A microphone is deep inside a half-buried drainpipe in a field as a farmer on a quad bike revs a tired diesel engine on a slope. Haphazardly, the side of a compost bin collapses, spilling leftover takeaway curry, half there, half gone onto a pair of nearly new brogues. The alarm stops. Rolls of damp pub carpet are thrown from the back of a moving van into a field. Clouds of black smoke form as idling diesel trucks line up in a holding shed. An uneven raining-down of guano inside a densely populated cave of bats early in the morning. We hear a man slowly running his finger along the top edge of a dusty picture frame depicting an image of a black boy staring in awe at jewels in a display case. A fight outside a pub recorded from inside the pub's large metal recycling bin is in the background. A bloodied pig bangs its head on a wall. Burgers fall off a barbeque in the left speaker while on the right speaker an apprentice is rodding a culvert, trying to get a nappy that was flushed down the toilet unstuck. He pokes and pokes in a jerky rhythm that we use as a template to give us the rhythm of what follows. The slide of warm lamb's fat into a blackened bucket. A fruit knife is used to try and scrape off scum round a bath. The blast of air, thick with dirt, slamming into lungs. There are limbs everywhere and alarms and pools of congealed fluids and engines going too fast, and sirens and no human voices. A cracked bottle of Spicebomb aftershave slides down a metal chute. Someone has their ear pressed to a small tube, trying to hear a conversation happening nearby. A wallet with little money in it but full of credit cards drops into a urinal at a concert.

Bulldozers, seagulls, a multitude of drowned-out voices. Grinding, cracking, torn plastic, mushy paper, rotten food and metal. Glass shards and broken wood. It gets louder.

Slurry from a pig farm is pumped through hoses in great arcs through the sky into lakes of shit everywhere in the world at the same time. Your own sewage flowing underground somewhere right now. A lawyer in the boot of a car unwittingly squishes their hand into some rotten fruit. The nibbling of a rat in a wall of a cheap restaurant. The sound of 8 million thuds of 8 million used disposable nappies into bins played out of Bluetooth speakers in different technology companies' boardrooms. Someone throws an important switch in a coal-fired power station in China. A skateboard whizzes through cat shit. A child kicks an empty plastic bottle on the ground at an impromptu migrant camp near

Calais. The grind and crunch as things collapse under the compactor in the hopper of a rubbish truck sped up and looped and sped up again, distorted. An outlet from a bromide plant bursts. A doctor scrapes her leftover kebab into a bin. A broom at speed along the floor of a huge commercial packing shed. The lid of a swing-bin for sharps in a prison's medical room swings lightly. A huge crack as a cruise ship splits its hull. At the exact same time, hundreds of miles away, a different crack as a tree root breaks through a rotting coffin. A wind of dust is coming, louder. It could be brake dust in a train tunnel, it could be ashes from a crematorium, it could be asbestos, it could be the dust from cluster bombs in Yemen, it could be the ash from someone burning incriminating evidence, it could be crushed cow bones, ground to a powder, it could be the end of an art project, it could be someone airing curtains from an abandoned house, it could be the embers from a lawyer burning the papers for former cases in his garden, it could be decorator's dust after sanding down stained floorboards. It swells and bites the microphone in tiny spikes. There's a worm in a rented eco-toilet that slides quietly around beneath. Now we're in the bins at the White House, rummaging around in the waste. Then an old bird's nest falls on a person's head in a loft in a shower of dust and dried grasses as an old already-broken egg hits the floor. A shudder of nylon carpet beneath a bar stool in Katowice. The collapse of a paper sick bag onto a mother's arms as she tries to rush it from the car to the bin.

Bulldozers, seagulls, a multitude of drowned-out voices. Grinding, cracking, torn plastic, mushy paper, rotten food and metal. Glass shards and broken wood. It gets louder.

Cows plunge through antiseptic baths at huge industrial ranches. Black ink in giant barrels pours into huge printers. A train toilet dumps its load accidentally while at a station. A jug of fermented cheese breaks and spills. Someone shovels fat in a sewer beneath an American diner-themed restaurant in the Philippines. A plastic pirate ship sinks in a thick red pond. Oil spills from everywhere. It is now behind the ears of people swimming, underneath the fingernails of people scrabbling in the mud, in the rapid blinking of the nictitating membranes on an Arctic tern, in the slap of a wave against a rock pool. A freezer is without power and all the body parts are defrosting. A hotel bath towel is mopping up spilt coffee. A teenager is giving birth in a slum.

Two weeks ago a rubbish truck delivered a single, full load of waste to a city dump. It has delivered the load to a specific, separate part of the dump. A child in bare feet has arranged every item, no matter how small, alphabetically and is now, one by one, saying the name of each object in her head, before passing it behind to her mother, who is either keeping it to one side in a box or putting it into a pile beside her.

The dust grows and grows. It's swirling now, recorded binaurally. It blends into the sound inside a ten-year-old bag of a never-emptied vacuum cleaner as it sucks up grit and cat hairs. It is now a roar, a rumble. We hear now from inside another vacuum cleaner, this time a handheld one sucking up bits of old food and stray Lego hands from underneath the child seat in a car. Then we're inside a hand dryer at a one-star hotel. Then we're inside the air-conditioning piping in the Channel Tunnel. Then we're inside the heating ducts of a temporary structure hosting a wedding for a TV celebrity. Then we're inside the chest of an asthmatic boy. Then we're inside the nearly finished dome at Chernobyl, listening to air being sucked out and recirculated through pipework. Now we're inside the exit pipe leading from a tumble dryer in a laundrette in Liverpool out of a window on the thirteenth floor. Now we're inside the throat of a smoker as they inhale on a pipe while watching the news in Gambia. Now we're inside a pair of bellows operated by an elderly man on his knees in front of a failing fire. Now we're inside a huge Catholic church organ as it starts to warm up and air passes. Now we're inside the nose of someone getting CPR. Now we're in a fan heater as it heats up a disabled person in a garden shed. Now we're inside a Malaysian Airlines jet engine at take-off. Now we're inside the fan on a laptop. Now we're by the ear of a sound engineer as she listens to the sound of wind whistling through the ribcage of a dead animal in the Highlands of Scotland. Now we're inside the fan of an ice-cream freezer in Israel. Now we're inside the chest of someone in the back of a lorry struggling to breathe. Now we're inside the cremation oven that may burn the body of Henry Kissinger. Now we're at a country fair, inside the pipework of a steam engine once used to run a cotton mill near Rochdale. Now we're in a van's ventilation system on the way back from the mines. Now we're the air leaving a football as it's kicked. Now we're in an extractor fan in the first-class toilet at 37,000 feet.

A mechanic is wading through a swamp full of old tyres and faded, floating Monster energy-drinks cans. A duck lands on a pond full of algae. A young woman washes her face from a filthy bowl. A terminally ill man trips over coming out of a laundrette and drops his new gloves in a puddle. Now a microphone placed inside a plughole beneath a communal men's shower block in Sonapur and one inside the bidet at the Palm Hotel. We listen to both at the same time. A pile of dirty laundry from a shelter is dumped in the back of a van. Piles of rotting brown fabric in greasy paper bags are stacked floor to ceiling and someone is pulling them down with a hook in clumps. Someone else walks into a spider's web in an old chicken barn and we hear the web crumple around their face. An artist has collected every takeaway cup of coffee or tea she has been given in the last ten years and built a house from it and is inside waiting for it to rot; we hear her laughing. Straw full of chicken droppings crackles and burns in an incinerator. A child soldier in Sudan puts a small stone in each ear.

Bulldozers, seagulls, a multitude of drowned-out voices. Grinding, cracking, torn plastic, mushy paper, rotten food and metal. Glass shards and broken wood.

The sound of a spider spinning silk into a web.

It's getting quieter.

We hear a lock turn. It is a padlock to a small cabinet in a jewellery shop. Then another, to a private bike store. Now a key turns in the door to a stationery cupboard in a stately home. A metal gate to a parking lot swings shut. The twizzle of a combination lock to open a safe containing sensitive government information. An alarm fob beeps. A hidden speaker buzzes as a glass door is opened by hand. Someone types a series of long passwords underneath what follows. A deadbolt is thrown across a large pitch-black wooden door as someone approaches. A car is locked remotely, a hundred latches are hooked, a thousand bolts are thrown, a million alarms are set. A prison guard lays her keys in a tray. A portcullis is lowered, a security pass bleeps as it touches a gate at Facebook headquarters. A large brass key is being cut. A metal detector makes a rising *woop* noise as a child passes through. Shutters on a shop front in Bond Street are closing rapidly.

A light rain shower. A slosh of a soaked sponge onto the windscreen of a Koenigsegg inside a hangar as someone starts to wipe soap bubbles away. There's a small creak as the central wiper is swung upwards and away from the glass. At that moment, a handful of diamonds are scattered in a thin-stemmed glass. Back to the slosh and wipe. All the fountains in all the shopping malls spurting on full power. The sound of the diamonds again. A hiss as the top of a glass bottle of imported sparkling water is opened. An elbow from a homeless person hits a car-showroom plate-glass window with a muffled boom. It's caught with a contact mic and the sound is then taken to a private cinema and played at full volume in surround sound but recorded from the projection booth. It stops rather abruptly as a pair of sunglasses is placed quietly down on a piece of raw Carrara marble. A glass slide is clipped under a microscope in a laboratory. A large, single, square ice cube circulates round the bottom of a whisky tumbler. Again and again. The whisky has all gone. Not realising it is closed, a dog runs into a greenhouse door. A man's wedding rings accidentally touches a revolving door as he pushes too hard on it. We follow him in through the turn and out the other side. Another boom from the homeless person's elbow. A maid is chiselling ice with a tool, but we just hear two downward scrapes. Someone else holds up a single-lens reflex camera to their eyes and their glasses touch the rear display screen with a light click. Ice round a different whisky tumbler. Then we are inside a cardboard box as Christmas decorations are piled up on top. They are wrapped in tissue paper, but we still hear the chink as they touch. This chinking gives a pitched tone to play with and it becomes a small melody. Over the rest of the piece of music, the tempo increases very slowly but significantly until by the end it is extreme. Now a person with brown skin is cleaning the side windows on a teak boat in a warm wind. The boat is moving in the choppy waters causing the ladder she is up to creak slightly. There is a child tapping on the glass of a large aquarium with a toy Nerf gun at roughly the same pace as the ladder creak. The taps from this are added into the groove with the Christmas decorations. A glugging of a whole bottle of red wine into a decanter has been turned from an audio file into a sample instrument to allow it to be played in pieces. A new slide slips under a microscope in a different lab. Another watch slips from a pocket onto changing-room tiles. A phone vibrates briefly on a glass office coffee table filled with International Klein Blue powder paint. Water drips off a model's beard onto a shiny surf-board in a TV studio. A child bumps their forehead gently on a window to a tool shop. Someone else is wiping a second cocktail glass with a towel. The wet rags of a window cleaner in a bucket, the slosh of a new mop, a hot flannel placed on a tray. A woman's watch, face up, is lightly dragged across a jeweller's counter. A bangle knocks against the brass and leather of a car door as the driver reaches down to pick up his dropped cigarette lighter. Police lights are spinning furiously; we hear them from the inside – not the siren, the mirrored reflectors hurtling round the light bulbs. An LED is blinking on a security panel and its tiny noise is amplified to the same level as the police lights. A security light pops on.

Bulldozers, seagulls, a multitude of drowned-out voices. Grinding, cracking, torn plastic, mushy paper, rotten food and metal. Glass shards and broken wood. It gets louder.

Someone is running through the sewers in Rome in bare feet. At the same speed, a windshield wiper on a Bell 525 helicopter is on its fastest setting even though the blades aren't spinning. This is our new tempo. A set of keys rattle on a polished wooden chair on a wooden launch boat tied to a pier. A busker's coins vibrate in a tin as a blacked-out motorhome goes past. A mother-of-pearl button on a coat rattles against the petrol tank of a motorbike. Cufflinks in a copper ashtray rattle as a ship pulls in to port. Bottles of brandy rattle against each other in the back of the boot of a rusty car travelling at high speed through the desert. The scooping of coins in a currency-exchange kiosk.

Twins are planning a stunt using a touchscreen, in which a pilot leaves a small plane mid-flight with no parachute and then follows it down as it descends rapidly. He would then climb back in and land it safely, but we just hear the tapping of their electronic pen on the screen, air conditioning and distant seagulls in the background.

An overhead fan is moving air about in a guest bedroom. A pair of hands on a woman's back. Fish swim idly in an aquarium in the same kind of quiet rhythm many thousands of miles away. We hear the ticking of many luxury watches in Switzerland, but filtered so we only hear the higher frequencies and the whole recording is laid in very gently. Two clubs in a golf bag in the back of an SUV are vibrating softly against each other as the car idles outside a fish restaurant. A bank of LCD TVs showing soundless images of a happy white couple in an apartment are buzzing and humming endlessly, but they're turned right down in the mix until you can barely notice them. A child at boarding school is gently exhaling her breath onto a cold windowpane. A long horn sound can be heard distantly through a closed, polished brass porthole and it loops all the way to the end of the piece.

Gold taps turning, gold teeth grinding, gold lifts rising, gold pens twisting, gold handles turning, gold curtains pulled shut.

It is getting quieter still beneath the horn, even though the sounds are stacking up. In a hotel room above a casino, a seventy-five-year-old man is putting in coloured contact lenses. A model looks at her reflection in an elevator as it moves slickly downwards. A

Murano glass vase is cooling in Venice, resting. A student is gently pouring a premixed cocktail into a glass in the back of a limousine while he waits for his sister. A candle wafts lightly in a restaurant bathroom. Someone is silently racking out lines of speed on a smoked-glass table. The shimmer of chandeliers in a train carriage at a station as a freight train goes past. An entire empty building made of glass still hums. In Florida, a bottle of Bling H2O is being carried shakily on a silver tray. On the same tray, a silver bucket full of Kentucky Fried Chicken. The stream of a millionaire's urine on ice cubes. An iPad is still showing a silent promotional movie at a security trade show, even though everyone has left. A picture taken from a magazine is pressed underneath glass at the framers. An iPhone on a plane is charging on a cashmere blanket as we hear someone trying a variety of white wines. A woman sniffs an unlit lavender-scented candle. Someone else is peeling tape off a just-renovated polished-stone kitchen work surface in one long seamless motion. Someone is admiring their name etched onto an office door by tracing their name with a finger. A Neighbourhood Watch sticker is being stuck against the glass pane in a front door. A vast see-through sculpture in a foyer, free of dust, shudders a little as a digger excavates foundations next door. A man is looking through binoculars at a box on a polished mahogany table, but we hear road noise. Someone else trips and drops a whole basket of handcreams on a sheepskin. Someone is changing the water in a vase of flowers. The ice-maker on a large fridge can't stop itself from grinding and crunching behind the scenes. A clunk as a bottle of perfume drops neatly into the dispensing slot of a vending machine in Milan at midnight. A steam room, teeth in a plastic tray, a pair of spurs and leather boots set down heavily by a kitchen door. The abrupt bang of a gavel. Two people in a shower.

Bulldozers, seagulls, a multitude of drowned-out voices. Grinding, cracking, torn plastic, mushy paper, rotten food and metal. Glass shards and broken wood. It's getting quieter.

An abandoned all-electric wedding car is almost silently idling. The screen of a diagnostics device in a hospital is flickering but not bleeping. A rifle sight repeatedly pressed against a cheek-bone in winter.

Someone in patent red shoes is bending over to pour wine. A stained-oak trophy cupboard is being carefully wiped. The muted flip of soft leather-soled slippers. A young girl is holding up a Diet Pepsi bottle and watching Netflix through it with the sound down. A key ring with various special fobs and a number of brass keys sits in a saucer that's shuffling slightly across the steel tabletop from the vibration of the dishwasher next door. An eye just pressed to a spy hole in a door. A bare foot on a glass-brick floor above a basement. A large undrunk smoothie poured softly down a sink. A heartbroken tailor with a pair of scissors cutting through skin accidentally. A bottle of blue pills in the bottom of a bag travelling at 4 mph. The glass in a shop window full of books below the flat of a chef preparing sushi shudders as a train passes beneath. A woman pushes a trolley on thick carpet and on it a cafetière chinks very faintly against porcelain. A lizard scuttles beneath a sunlounger. The distant rattle of test tubes on trolleys elsewhere. The purr of liquid nitrogen across stones. A man swishing liquor backwards and forwards in his mouth, lips closed. A large telescope pointing up to space shifts on ball bearings hidden in the base as it's swung round by someone in a swimsuit. One thousand perfume bottles in a factory shuffle forward in a row at the end of a shift. A baby monitor; something is happening in the background now. A pool seen from the top floor of a building by an au pair sending WhatsApp messages. Smash – a football through the glass of a kitchen window. Something hurtling down a gravel drive sped up until all 500 metres of it is condensed into one-and-a-half seconds. A full kettle is boiling unwatched and steaming up the mirrors backstage. Someone else is hurling gym equipment through a windscreen. A car is rampaging through duty free on YouTube. A rifle has been shot through a conservatory at the same time as a bottle of commun-ion wine is thrown through a stained-glass window. A tower of jars of relish in a delicatessen tumbles forwards. A boy scout staggers backwards through a window. An AV system corrupts and starts playing the sound of a trans person destroying a Blu-ray player with a hammer rather than the graduation scene on the Blu-ray disc it should be playing. A musician is throwing pairs of champagne glasses out of the toilet window at a fashion party. A cargo plane full of Chinese pottery hits turbulence. Brown water starts spluttering from a gold tap as someone tries to run a bath. A policeman steps on a phone by accident and cracks the screen. A dentist slips and drills into an inflamed gum. A key snaps off in a lock. A diving mask fills up with salty water. A fountain pen leaks ink onto a striped shirt as someone bends down to wipe their shoes with a tea towel. A whisky tumbler slips. A dishwasher starts spraying water everywhere from a broken hose. A kid throws a cup of diluted juice over a wall of art works. A teenager pukes in his father's bed.

An ice cube splits. An ice shelf cracks.

Bulldozers, seagulls, a multitude of drowned-out voices. Grinding, cracking, torn plastic, mushy paper, rotten food and metal. Glass shards and broken wood.

A recording of a huge group of cleaners and domestic staff walking together through a city, banging wood and metal, played so loudly out of speakers next to an empty tall glass building that parts of it start to fragment, to shatter into a million tiny pieces.

It gets louder.

8.

Presto

To digest

A polio doctor in Pakistan, on a break from work, sits at a small green wooden table with colleagues and picks up a knife and fork. From nowhere we hear the swift, overly hurried and deferential whoosh of a pair of automatic glass doors to a supermarket opening. Early in the morning somewhere a stray cat purrs at a baker's feet. We hear the slow slide of a peeling, laminated menu across the surface of a dirty linoleum-topped table. The ping of a push bell as a cook, having plated up, is ready for service. By a small stream, someone under a tree is using a clear, hollow, plastic, sharpened toothpick, picking at their teeth in regular high-pitched clicks and ticks. In between, the sound of 328 English Aga lids closing in the gaps. A buttering of overly stiff brown toast at a roadside café is simplified to a few quick sweeps of the knife in a triplet figure. On the last scrape, a frozen leg of mutton falls on the floor of a speeding van with a bang. It is answered by the ritualistic sucking-out of flesh from a cherimoya fruit by a series of angry Republicans. Different brands of ketchup squirt from unbranded plastic bottles at the same time. Someone unwittingly stands on a ripe plum on the floor of a warehouse. A maid drops a duck egg from a cotton-lined woven basket on the dark-timbered floor of a holiday cabin near Phuket. As if in answer, we hear a unison dong as different people in different places try to break an egg on the rim of a medium-sized Pyrex bowl, though their contact on the side of the bowl is not hard enough and none of their eggs break. Consequently we just hear the ringing dong sound as their eggs strike different bowls in many kitchens in several different countries exactly at once. Each one is placed in a different position in the stereo image to create a kind of cocoon-like reverberant bell sound. This sound drenched in a long metallic plate reverb.

An elderly butler drops a heavy coloured-crystal wine glass on the polished teak deck of a boat. It is answered by 65,000 traditional Portuguese corks being pulled out of vintage French red-wine bottles at the same time. A full jar of hot marmalade is dropped on a traditional quarry-tiled floor by a sugar-beet farmer in Norfolk, followed immediately by fizzy drinks from a SodaStream in Israel being rapidly siphoned into different-sized bottles. This siphoning moves over the space of five seconds. From the fizz emerges the sound of Sainsbury's Taste the Difference bacon in a hot frying pan recorded with great care and attention by Peter Cobbin, senior engineer at Abbey Road, using up to twenty-two microphones. We enjoy all the minute variations and detail of its sizzle. As the fat spits with increasing urgency, we become aware of another spitting sound fading underneath – a new batch of bratwurst sausages on the grill at Meister Bock at Cologne Station, but recorded on a phone. Someone has tried to engrave a recording of a pig being killed onto a tortilla and is playing it on a record player. A member of the Cargill family is quietly tearing off a piece of Domino's pepperoni pizza, a lawyer is eating steamed bread in prison, but we can't quite hear either. Instead we hear a single, loud, curt gesture: the crushing of garlic under a thick knife in the kitchen of a small motorhome as punctuation. Then scissors snipping the end off a smallish plastic-sealed tube of liver pâté on a beach and a repeated regular stabbing with a fork of the plastic cover to a ready meal by a nurse on a night shift. On the last of the punctures, and exactly in time, a mechanic slips and accidentally bangs a wrench against a large empty copper vat at the Heineken factory in Amsterdam. It makes a big, echoey, metallic clang which we hear dying away beneath the road noise.

An aeroplane is overhead. An alcoholic kitchen porter at a private function on Kellogg Drive, VA sharpens chef's knives in quick succession; we hear just a tiny excerpt of each but played at speed. A sugar lump drops on a small metal tray. This sound is heard again, but played out of speakers at high volume into a shipping container. Its echo can be heard in an anonymous cavernous space nearby. An empty can of malt drink is crushed by a Caterpillar-branded boot, sharply cutting off the reverb tail of the previous sound. A near-empty tea urn at a village fête far away is gurgling, ticking underneath. A cherry spat into a chipped white enamel dish with blue edges overlaid. A hand rests on another smaller hand, stirring a pot on a stove with a crude wooden spoon. A huge metal colander is dropped in a stainless-steel sink at the development kitchen of a well-known restaurant. A laptop, its screen opened on a recipe, is dragged across an expensive antique table. A close-up of a not-yet-ripe Palestinian lemon's skin and pith being peeled with a hand-held zester tool; not a big sound, but it's still there, only noticeable when it stops, a presence afraid of an absence. Grind, grind: a salt mill. A grandmother is crushing golden rice in Dehradun in an iron pestle and mortar that was given as a wedding gift. It crossfades into the sound of an almond-grading machine near Modesto in California. We hear the almonds bounce and trickle quickly through the slatted metal grille. Now we hear the vibrating sound at the end of a conveyor belt inside a giant flour mill, recorded from above. A pause.

A breakdown: every pot on every stove in the world making popcorn right now, and the kernels are popping. Not dedicated popcorn-making machines and their whirring, clumsy mechanics; just pots on stoves, lids on. The recordings with the noisiest backgrounds are mixed the most quietly so the sound of the pots and popcorn is foregrounded. Consequently there is an accumulation of temporary stillness as people around these pots wait for the kernels to pop. There will be a few recordings with excited chatter from children nearby, but again we want to feel anticipation rather than be distracted by language, so any recordings with audible words on have been turned down in volume until they're unrecognisable or the talking edited out. Assuming we are listening in on just pots and stoves whose oil is about to reach the right temperature (and eliminating those that have already started popping), this beginning lasts 10,144 milliseconds from no pops to all done. There should be a natural crescendo as we listen to every pot and stove until every corn has popped. Each of the recordings or live microphones stops at the precise moment the last corn has popped on the individual pan it is recording. Because some will be cooked before others, the effect is to feel a natural thinning-out from a dense barrage of popping to infrequent single pops and bursts until we are left with just one kernel to pop inside just one pot.

We begin again. The crack of 40 per cent of the total stock of Lidl bananas having their necks broken, ready to be peeled, the sounds piled up on top of each other. To help blur it into the next sound, a little tape delay added. The feedback knob on the tape delay is set at around 70 per cent, so the sound keeps moving on and on. It begins to fade out as we hear the slow breaking, opening of a too-ripe Australian avocado skin with a single curve of the knife. A sheep stands while it has a number twenty-one sprayed on its back. A trainee chef picks herbs in a forest. A boxcutter skilfully punctures the plastic seal round a barrel of brominated vegetable oil in a long slicing motion. Then in various kitchens across Europe, finely chopped shallots hit the bottom of hot pans roughly at the same time. Some cookery books are piled on a fire. There's a rapid stacking of dirty dishes. A windscreen on a food truck in San Francisco shatters. An olive plops into a martini. Now the slow peeling-back of a small Spanish tin of anchovies down the middle of the stereo image is automated so it gets louder and louder as the stereo image turns inward to mono, a diminuendo. A brushing of hair behind an ear near a fire; a sharp knife lingers through an octopus; another olive in another martini. Then back in again in haste with everything colliding on top of itself. A half-empty barrel of balsamic vinegar sloshes around on the shoulder of a woman in Perugia. A washing of fresh, damp parsley from a garden in Provence. Laid over the top, a sifting of genetically modified cornflour, a flicked pan of peanuts, gluey fingers sticking to a packet of crisps, the trembling opening of a couscous packet, the pouring of Karol, sixty-seven people trying to eat mussels in silence. A shaken packet of hot sugared doughnuts at a fairground. A slam of frozen chips into a fryer in a van parked outside Berghain nightclub in Berlin. A Spanish peach stone spat into an empty rainwater barrel. A partner of a miner drops a plate of pap and vleis. An empty blender joins in, but it's not actually a blender, it's a dentist's drill recorded in Guadalajara slowed down to resemble a food mixer. It slows down further, the whole track now sucked in behind it. A stream of vomit from a lead singer in detox. Someone else quickly eats two packets of chocolate biscuits in a bedroom in double time. Then off again. A crate of empty Coke bottles slammed down outside the back of a small café beneath a hydroelectric dam, answered by someone choking on a piece of steak. The sound is cut short by the crack of a dry organic oatcake being snapped by an embarrassed painter-decorator. The angry crackle of fat on a bit of industrial bacon on a campfire. A faulty extractor fan in a mountain lodge above a smoking, sticking fondue. A large bottle of thousand-island dressing falls off a table in Texas but doesn't smash. The suck of separate teats from a milking machine on cows' udders in a huge shed. The tumble of empty Roundup barrels in a pickup truck in Ha Giang. The dumb suck of an early-seventies chest-freezer lid opening, breaking its seal, itself interrupted by sixteen packets of crisps being stamped on in quick succession – each one a different flavour. Teetering boxes of wedding cakes cascade off the edge of a loading bay. A ripe tomato hits a politician on the back of their neck. A man slurps a prawn. Now the small squeak of human teeth against a too-thick, out-of-date slice of lightly grilled halloumi recorded in a studio in front of a live audience. Then immediately spat in a bin. The dull mini thuddish crack as you bite into a sour cherry expecting it to be sweet and also thinking that the stone has gone but finding too late that it isn't and biting too hard on it. It's a sound that comes again and again in what follows. A lemon tree uprooted. A child bites through a solid R White's Lemonade ice lolly but doesn't swallow. A quail's egg dropped suddenly on a Delaware marble floor put through a reverb mapped from a huge indoor Polish pig shed just after all the pigs have been loaded onto a lorry. The slow long scrape of a Star Wars-themed ice-cube tray against the side of the freezer compartment of a fridge as the tray is removed. The sound slows down in time, but the pitch remains the same. It is as if the world goes into slow motion. This stretching of scraping ice eventually comes to a pause, a kind of hover. Gallons of blood pour onto the floor. A tanker in a traffic accident is spilling its cargo of milk. An industrial orange juicer is churning in Brazil. A thundering of taps filling washing-up bowls across the world. A series of underwater microphones record the rip of commercial dredging along the seabed. A Krispy Kreme executive is pissing in the shower. A mic inside the radiators of all the engines of all the Waitrose lorries on the M25 right now, even if they are stationary. The blood is still pouring. An unnoticed phone is vibrating on a messy kitchen table. A forklift idling in an apple cold store at Scripps Farm in Kent. A single gas-burner ring on full with nothing on the stove. The doctor stabs a pakora with her fork. This echoes within an unlit hollow, wooden space.

All the kitchens cooking school dinners start to roar about this time, arranged according to the price per head, starting with the most expensive first. They pile in on top of each other quickly. By the end, it is cacophonous. It finishes with a huge tray of cheap frozen sausage rolls sliding into a giant open oven. Exactly at the end of this sound, the first Russian vodka bottle in an empty but huge recycling bin in Tbilisi strikes a hollow metallic ring.

Now the beating-out of air from a pig's lungs by an alcoholic butcher at four o'clock in the morning comes in hard, a new tempo. Twelve cows, one after another, having numbers clipped to their ears. A beer-bottle top in Nigeria is pulled off by a singer's teeth. Now teeth being pulled out of piglets' jaws. A waiter in Monrovia slams down a tray full of burgers, fries, coleslaw – answered by 21,100 diabetics in America either pulling a ring-pull or twisting the lid off a pressurised bottle one after another in furious succession. Even at considerable speed, this will take time to play out, the horror in the repetition. At its end, it trips into more lungs being beaten, lungs, lungs. A slit throat. A furious mixing of icing, by hand, in a bowl. Three tight chops through a neck of celery on a chopping board. Blocks of hydrogenated vegetable oil drop in the boot of a salesman's car with a thud. A salad spinner spins freely as, with the tiniest of plops, nail clippings drop into a bowl of soup someone is about to eat. Now a rolling boil inside a hospital kitchen in Aleppo at night – interrupted by blanched potatoes hitting hot duck fat in a pan on a TV cookery show 4,252 miles away. A cork from a bottle of single-malt whisky on a British Airways flight. The jingly hop and splosh of a supermarket trolley into a canal is squeezed shorter, putting it all on a single beat. It punches the piece up, down. A stop. Two snappings of fresh Yorkshire carrots brings it back in. A lemon squeezed, pigs burned, bitter cherries bitten, teeth pulled, syringes thrown into a metal bowl with a ringing sound. A finger broken, snapped off, snaps in. The cruel grind of an arm through a machine – but gone again. A dry cracker eaten, an energy drink opened, a boat capsizes as an indeterminable hum beneath; celery snapped. A stop. A tractor reversing over a body crossfades into the fall of rain on king-prawn ponds in Vietnam at night. We luxuriate in this sound for a while. But then a toaster pops up, ready. There's nothing in it. A food mixer twirls boringly on a film set. Inside, dough for chocolate brownies with the wrong combination of ingredients. An insistent, anxious door buzzer to a food bank in Newport recorded from the inside. Men stuff hot dogs in their mouths at an eating competition. An empty Cornish-pasty packet skates over the surface of a footpath at a stately home and it's mic'd up by someone following and running along-side it, keeping up and pausing when necessary. Many bellies rumble, unheard by each other. The chicken you haven't eaten yet, but will appear on a menu you will be offered in the next few weeks, is just hatching alongside 24,999 other chickens right now in a commercial hatchery. There are hums of industrial heaters and a multiplicity of tiny identical cheeps, creating an almost singular tone. Over the top of this sound comes something that almost sounds like a bonfire crackling, but is in fact Chinese takeaway staff gently filling a paper bag with just-hot prawn crackers. Crossfade into a child unwrapping the plastic of a seaweed-and-rice triangle from a Lawson store in Osaka. The tentative unwrapping of a squashed cheese-and-pickle sandwich wrapped in foil on top of a small mountain. A blowtorch on an amateur brûlée is quietly at the back of the mix. An unopened bagged salad is tossed in a cardboard box. Someone unknown forcibly breaks an olive-oil breadstick backstage in the green room at a Beethoven concert. A blueberry Innocent smoothie squirts onto a crisp white shirt. A glug of blood from a neck. Any Italians in any restaurant at the moment, snapping grissini at the same time. A single anonymous wrist snaps beneath the weight of a tower of stacked wooden crates, followed by the lids of 1 million rice cookers closing. We hear dim-sum steaming baskets placed softly but jerkily on a table; beneath it the hubbub in a canteen at a Red Bull factory, laid over someone trying to spread soft cheese on a cracker while lying in a hospital bed, laid over someone quietly sifting icing sugar, laid over a smallholder hoeing their vegetable patch, laid over the draining of spaghetti in a retirement home, laid over a distant vicious crumpling of the plastic tray from a Jaffa Cakes packet heard from the room next door, laid over a slow stirring of mint tea, laid over the laying-out of crisps, laid over the slow peeling-back of foil on a large, own-brand coleslaw tub, laid over a tray sliding across a stone floor, laid over a minibar door-shudder, laid over a child fishing for pickles from a jar – the sounds each having their moment before settling back into the general landscape of sounds.

Softly now: the bubbling of fish tanks; inside, drowsy turtles piled on top of each other. A vast vat of oil coming to temperature in a factory recorded with a hydrophone inside. Still quietly, a huge container ship slowly turns up its engines, ready to leave. A kettle backstage at a crematorium boils and can't turn itself off. Inside every dishwasher working at this moment we hear sloshing and churning recorded from the inside. A hook and float is cast into a still pond. A continuous pouring of wine. Someone has dug up all the lids of takeaway cups of coffee or tea buried in the ground in the nineties from a landfill site near you. Barbecues are being lit, barbecues are being thrown away. A colossal clatter of pans from restaurants in Sri Lanka; many people are furiously flipping and shuffling a hot wok right now on a stove. Someone's hand slips on a cheese grater and grates through the skin on their knuckles instead. A barrel of beer from a lorry to a cellar. Workers are running through an orchard. Bones dropped on a tray. A hedgehog bites through dry cat food left outside. A pig bites on a peach stone. Chickens peck at grain in a metal feeder in the same rhythm as the banging-out of used coffee grinds in Brooklyn coffee shops. A man scrapes an unfinished bowl of organic porridge, honey and flax seed onto a compost heap. Trucks everywhere reversing up to landfill sites, emptying their guts into holes. And the dragging of chairs and tables across floors and carpets, and the tearing of napkins, and spilt water, and the crumpling of plastic cups, and the folding of paper plates. The clasping of hands for grace. A bolt through the head of a male calf. A single onion falls out of a shopping bag in a car park with a bonk.

Someone on their own is snapping a large bar of chocolate in the dark. A home-delivery lorry out bringing food to a neighbour slams its door. A pizza delivery helmet lands on a warm pizza box. A cook slices through a finger. A strawberry picker is struggling to breathe by the side of a road. Over the top is layered the sound of a person who doesn't know they are seriously ill yet, peeling back the blue plastic lid of a lunchbox. A milk bottle smashes on rough concrete. A machine for slicing ham switches on and comes to speed quite quickly. We hear the blade mechanism slide towards where the ham is clamped in place. It's a short sound, but it's enough for us to anticipate the sound that is coming – the metallic whizz of the circular blade losing its shine as it slices through breaded, salted flesh. Frozen mice are defrosting ready to be fed to a pet snake.

In the distance we hear a short rung bell calling children in from the fields to eat and then a version of silence: an empty suburban supermarket on the edge of a typically sized Ukrainian town with its lights off. Except we realise there is a significant humming. The fridges and freezers are still on. It is unrecognisable yet familiar, a place in limbo, in mourning, in waiting – a magic place where every shelf produces every conceivable food you could want, regardless of the season, the country of origin or the distance travelled to get there. We need the whole place to hum for us to know it was once alive itself, to feel we can survive, and we listen to its unpleasant, discordant drone for some time. Something is changing, though; slowly we feel like we're moving towards the fridges – maybe the one in the cold meats aisle – but in fact it is a fading-up of a fridge in another supermarket somewhere close by. Then, one by one, a single fridge from each supermarket within a ten-mile radius is added to the sound, sonically stacked on top of each other, placed in a location binaurally or simulated to represent its position on a map, one after another. The hum now is pretty loud, but we've only just got started. The radius is widened and every three seconds, using the criteria of distance – closest to the location of the original fridge, another fridge is added from another supermarket, and another, and another until every fridge in every supermarket that is on right now is heard on top of each other in a giant, violent, thuggish, bellicose chorus. We hear that sound at high volume for fifty seconds. Suddenly it stops. The sound of a lamb you may choose to eat or not to eat is currently grazing; we hear its teeth pulling and tearing the grass. Quietly it is augmented by the pulling-off of a lid of a yoghurt pot, black-cherry-flavoured, by a nun. An empty Snickers drink rolls to the right-hand side of a bus on the top floor. The sped-up rattling of shopping trolleys, separated in haste. The catch of a Kilner biscuit-jar lid being popped. A diabetic child with her ear near a bowl of Ricicles. The spit of cheap chicken on a long grill. A murderer's last meal served in a plastic dish. A hurried can opener on a tin of own-brand chicken-flavoured cat food. A microwave ping, answered by however many microwaves are pinging right now in unison, mixed with tape delays and reverb. A brisk stirring of low-calorie sweetener in a cup of tea at the Foreign Office. A plate set firmly and unkindly on the floor. The hiss of the skin of an arm burned on an oven shelf. The fridges again, maxed out over the rattling of trolleys, a sub rumble throughout. The flip of a single pair of slippers; it is 3 a.m. Flip, flip, flip. This is our metronome. All else is measured by this flip, flip, flip. The click of the snap of a photographer's bag on his way back from a South American farm. The grinding of the teeth of a farm worker made to stand there and grin for a packaging image. The whack of a coconut on a head. Flip. The careful washing of chickpeas in a filthy stream. Flip. The potato-picking machine breaks down with a bang. Flip. A tiny excerpt of the laying of plates at a buffet for a driving instructors' conference. Flip. The tank behind a greenhouse mixing a blend of water, chemicals and nutrients for the violently green basil plants next door. Flip. The pulling of weeds by a road in Yemen. Flip, thud. The noise of a truck driver sitting down on a toilet by a motorway. Flush. The miserable semi-din of orange lights inside Thanet Earth. Flip. A phone rings from Monsanto to fulfill a re-order. Flip, peel, pop, the stickering by hand of the specials stickers at the end of the day in a corner of a shop in Bergen. Flip. Running water into a duck pond. Bang: a dairy farmer throws files in a removals box. Bang: a gunshot over a field. Hush: the slaves on Thai fishing boats are sitting quietly, nearly silent, so we just hear the churn of the boat's engine as it heads out to sea again. Two hundred chickens are stunned with electrodes, a new kind of noise they've not made before. The fearful flapping of 2,000 fish in a net resting on the bottom of a boat. Two hundred thousand pigs in gas chambers. The bodies of animals tumbling into bins. A van full of labourers chugs out fumes next to the café while they wait for the driver to finish his coffee. A metal spatula scrapes mince too vigorously off a Teflon pan. A lawyer is typing a lawsuit. Eggs being collected from metal-grilled trays for the mayonnaise in the tuna sandwich at the petrol station on the road to school. The rattle of tins of mints in handbags. The crates being loaded. The lorries arriving, the ships turning, the planes landing, water gushing through pipes. A bee is stuck inside the plastic sheeting of a polytunnel. At the same time a makeup artist for Gordon Ramsay gets a text message from her boyfriend during the taking of pictures for an advertising shoot. The squeak of the gate as it's opened to let the cows pass on their last day in Herefordshire. The squeak is slowed down a lot and looped underneath the tiny sound of the pinning of hairnets in a factory.

The sound of dripping water nearby but not inside the crude hut of the worker who is currently picking the fruit you'll see in the shop next week. The sliding-back of a resealable top on a bag full of grated Red Leicester cheese by a nine-year-old boy. A timer goes off by a KFC frying station. A manager bites a crumbly wafer over his dessert on a date with the wine buyer. Plastic corks bobble en masse into landfill. An out-of-date packet of chapatis hits the bottom of a plastic bin. All the zips of all the packed lunch bags as their contents are about to be eaten. A Chorleywood bread-factory fire alarm goes off. The lumpen shudder of a hidden toy in a shaken cereal box. The sound of six beers in a cardboard sleeve hitting the bottom of the trolley. A lobster split in two down the middle with a sharp knife. The hidden jangle of a small, cheap, whisky bottle against loose change in someone's pocket. A mic inside the crates and crates of bourbon in the back of a lorry on a ferry, pulling in, rattling furiously in time with the engine. The coffee-stall grinder, the coffee farmer coughing. The shuffle of a cashier's feet under the table. The packing up of a local grocer for good. The simple dull thwack of frozen croissants on baking tins. The synthetic apricot-scented freshener squirting automatically in the toilet of a museum's cafe. The purr of dialysis. The scanner of an in-store shopper, buying something for the online shopper, bleeps once. The felling of a rare tree, sped up. A passing of blood-red urine. A paper mill at full pelt mixed beneath. A bleep from the dialysis machine. Ink-making and printing. A half-full plastic water bottle forcefully kicked. A sewing-up of bruised flesh alongside the rapid breathing of a hidden migrant. The rows of hung haddock as they get dipped in dye and liquid smoke. The dinner lady trips over the chemo trolley. The ice-cream van reversing into a docking bay and hitting the side of a caravan by mistake. The throwing and unloading of frozen turkeys at dawn. The abattoir worker blowing on a hot chocolate on a break during the night shift. The out-of-breath shopper bending down to pick up a tin of meatballs in tomato sauce. The plastic tablecloth wiped free of crumbs. The gloop of caramel in a bowl over a pan of boiling water for the second time. But now everyone puking up alcohol. Millions of children at a birthday party about to eat sausage rolls at the same time. An insulin injection in the toilet at a diet-industry conference. The squeak of two polystyrene boxes rubbing against each other at Billingsgate. A cute pig squeal. A failed harvest of corn, cracking slightly in the heat. The spitting of burning butter in pans. A manufacturer has set out rows of tasting pots and we hear the sound of the sales agent washing their hands next door. An amputation. The daughter of an asparagus farmer in Peru is at the back of a small classroom flicking her teeth with a branded plastic pen. A wild pony bites on a discarded Pink Lady apple core on the side of a steep hill. A fisherman drops a large red string bag of whelks on the harbour wall, but it splits and spills its contents on the tarmac. Another tree felled for paper which will later be used for the menu of the nearest Indian restaurant, sped up at least double speed. As it hits the ground, a huge spray of pig shit from a waste lagoon onto fields. A huge bong again, this time from inside an empty oil tanker at a dock in Colombo as it's about to refill and the pipe is connected. From this expanse of sound comes another: in Dubai, leftover noodles from the breakfast buffet at the Sofitel is scraped into a large black bin liner, the knife making a squeal against the porcelain as it does so. This screech is given a long reverb, mapped from an impulse response of an empty parliament building, and in it we can distantly hear chains along a dock, a carcass dragged along the floor, a bag of genetically modified potatoes pulled through a chip-shop kitchen, a buffalo hide through long grass, a shaking of Crunchy Nut Cornflakes into bowls, a vivid mechanical whisking of egg whites for a birthday pavlova in Vienna, a pulverising of gristle, a constant avalanche of brightly coloured wrapped sweets down a roller ramp towards a huge, wheeled crate, a sliding-off of plastic from several long baguettes at once, a continuous suction of blood, fluid and fat in a liposuction operation, a loud pouring of water like a sieve from the nets on the back of a fishing boat as it hauls in an illegal catch, a fan whirring, keeping lights cool above a table on which sits a perfect plastic curry, an apple-polishing machine in South Africa churning furiously, the continuous but gentle grinding of spices by hand in prison, two soon-to-be-peeled buckets of shrimp pulled along the floor by a child in a dust mask in Phuket, a giant combine harvester spilling commercially trademarked grain into a giant truck, rain on a tin roof on a shack on a farm, a continuous slice down the chest of a cow, any cow, the spraying of Calypso insecticide, a vacuum cleaner sucking up pistachio shells from underneath a table in Las Vegas, a suicide bomb exploding in a food market.

A chef washes sinew off her hands. Air-sealed blocks of kebab meat in bags, punctured, releasing the air from inside with a sigh. Cans of soup falling from the top of a building and splitting open in sharp succession on the pavement. Bottle tops pinging off the top of imported beers and hitting the metal ducting above. Bakery tins crashing onto the empty metal sheets lower down. A bottle of Lucozade hurled through the window of a hospital. Aerosols of cheap cream are squirting in short, short stabs upwards. Frozen turkeys are melting in the heat from a supermarket fire, the plastic of their packaging moulding to the skins. Shelves collapse, crushing bags of organic dried fruit in small green pouches. Yoghurt starting to ferment, normalised, made loud. Pastry cracking open. Mould growing. A farmer slamming the phone down on a buyer. Many packets of dried grains trembling on a shelf in an earthquake, recorded from inside each packet. The angry pop of a lid off a glass jar of curdled vanilla cream. Lettuce washed and dragged through chlorine. All the batteries are leaking, burning. The splosh and thud of wellies through a field as a farmer's daughter looks at a ruined crop of beetroot. Thousands of green potatoes bouncing unevenly down several flights of graffitied stairs. One or two empty hangers bumping into each other inside a makeshift wardrobe as a train goes overhead while a pot-washer cleans his teeth for work. A rogue bottle of Dr Pepper rolling sideways during a shootout with police. Salad bags popping with force. All the tills in American food shops are bleeping at once now, you can hear them here, you know what it is. It's happening right now. DVDs of all unwatched food programmes in anti-cancer charity shops are stacked vertically in their cases and cracking under the weight. Vitamin pills and protein supplements are rattling in small plastic tubs in a trade box in the back of an estate car. The pouring of sweeteners and protein powders like a waterfall over a pyramid of neatly stacked quinoa packets. Sewage can be heard running from a pipe, but at some distance across a field. The thump of an unripe Somali mango along an uneven wooden floor knocks a black poison box by the back door. The slow slip of oil down the back of a shelf. The airy wind of custard powder, mustard powder tipping graciously off shelves joins the dusty cascade. All the rolls of foil unravelling, unravelling across miles and miles out of the doors of all the shops. On the back of a moped, pieces rattling inside packets inside wrapped presents for the child of a waiter at a hotel where you will visit. A venomous spider in a crate of bananas travelling at high speed out of sight in the dark. The hungry peeling-back of mouldy sandwiches in one violent gesture. A volcano of broken biscuits that failed the quality testing at the factories. The snap of a trap on a rat as it goes for bait on the floor of a kitchen you ate in. The rattle of single-use cutlery by teenagers on a date. Someone pouring milk powder on a fire to make a fireball; a puncture in the bottom of a can of Stella causing a tiny but fierce fountain over the shoes of a commuter. Sparkling flavoured water all over the floor, fizzing desperately. Frozen peas in their billions melting slowly in the packets, recorded from the inside. Plastic, plastic, plastic, plastic, plastic, plastic, plastic. Every cheap kettle boiling at once next to cups ready with teabags. A coffee bean explodes politely on a small pan by a tent. A showering-down of broken glass from corporate headquarters. The firm peeling-back of skin from a rabbit caught in a homemade trap next to an open fire in woodland. Toilet rolls going up quickly with a *woomph*; the sprinklers are supposed to be on but we can only hear one working. The heat is making the jars of pickle and sauces explode with a muted crack. An anorexic dancer on the set for an ad about exercise breaks her leg with a bitter, heavy snap. A sister shakes a box of grape nuts. A fly keeps landing on the same bit of abandoned meat at the counter. The crumbling of Rennies, Gaviscon. All the bottled waters thrown off shops' shelves at once. San Pellegrino. Vittel. Highland Spring. Evian. Volvic. GLACÉAU Smartwater. Aqua Pura. Nestlé Pure Life. Badoit. Brecon Carreg. Dasani. Mount Franklin. Morning Fresh. Oro. Buxton. Poland Spring. Perrier. Radenska. Spa. Souroti. Trump Ice. Aqua Safe. Some bottles smash, some bobble awkwardly, some do nothing. There's something in this shop that gives you cancer and it makes a noise here. Everything in the freezer sounds like it is coming alive. In fact, it is recordings of the life cycle of every animal or bit of an animal now frozen inside the freezer condensed into a one-minute chunk and played out of speakers hidden at the bottom.

A basket held by a young boy bangs the corner of an aisle. We hear the sound of the popcorn again. A maize-farm worker in Kenya is being sprayed with pesticide by a tractor as it passes between the trees. An airline meal is plonked down in front of you. A young person is retching quietly, hunched over a school toilet. Bleep: your bananas through the scanner. Someone nervously fiddling with coins in a queue, trying to work out if they have enough money to buy the thing they need to eat. A dog with a bone, a cat with a bird in its mouth. A thin child chewing on dried pasta. Someone about your age, similar height, not far from where you grew up, walks into a restaurant. A crashing of over-stuffed waste bins. Just as her colleagues break out in laughter at her story, the doctor raises her fork and opens her mouth.

9.

Sostenuto

To work

Under harsh spotlights a worker – dark-skinned, thin, tired and immobile – has his head cocked back, looking up at the cabin of a crane in silence while another worker snips the ends of cable ties nearby. It is hot with barely any wind and just past midnight. Nobody is bothering to pick up the long, discarded tips of the black plastic ties. There are no radios on and no speaking or singing, but there are constant interruptions of bangs, power tools and engines. The recording is unlikely to contain birdsong. He clears the dust from his throat again.

An assistant is adjusting the legs of a tripod in the dark. An artist is mixing paints for a background in a title sequence.

A woman is washing bed sheets by hand in the moonlight in the left speaker. On the right, a few kilometres away from her, we hear a garment bag being unzipped, slowly. On the left, the rumble of a tank under a bridge; on the right, a Namibian is pumping water from a poisoned well without any light. On the left someone is writing racist tweets in a small room with no windows, on the right someone is upstairs in an elaborate Halloween costume on her own, stirring a hot chocolate. On the left police are dragging someone drunk to the cells. On the right someone from the local council is turning the lights off on a high street. On the left some-one is sipping from a cocktail in bed while the person next to them is snoring; on the right, the horn from a huge cargo ship a significant distance away in thick fog recorded across the water from land. On the left, a sheet being pulled over a face; on the right, the boot of a taxi opens with a squeak at midnight. On the left, a bristle of paperwork into a folder; on the right, a fax spitting out a death threat into an empty office.

The tearing of gaffer tape beneath a table with a single microphone set up on the top. The waving of a huge, unwashed bed sheet to sound like a flag in a Foley studio.

On the left we hear the small pop of a lid removed from lipstick by someone skinny next to a chest of drawers. On the right a miner underground takes a small bite from a rotten apple core by the dying light of his head torch. On the left a lawyer doesn't know if it's day or night but is twisting and turning on a metal bed with her eyes closed. On the right someone is underneath a car attaching a small dark box by the light of a key-ring torch. In stereo now, two Australian girls are skinny dipping in the Maldives by moonlight and we hear them make weird noises under the water as we record them from above as they try to come up for air.

A piano tuner opens his briefcase. A steward in thick glasses tears tickets.

A person is supervising the unloading of coal in North Korea using repeated short blasts on a plastic whistle. Someone is shooting magpies across a field using only a torch as light. A researcher is in a small, hastily built hide covered in grasses and is writing a diary, unaware of the cracking sounds happening behind her. An army recruit is face down in damp dirt inside the hollowed-out remains of a fallen tree. A bedroom door is broken down while twins sleep as fire spreads and burns in the rooms above. People in a forest are chainsawing Christmas trees off at the base of the trunks. An electrician walks towards a dark figure with a candle across a meadow. A clean-shaven man is unbuttoning his shirt in a dingy hotel room in Buenos Aires with his phone tucked under his chin.

A big production meeting for a new piece of musical theatre on Broadway is interrupted by the sound of a news alert appearing on the director's phone. An editor knocks a pair of glasses off a table onto the floor with his elbow.

A fake snow machine is turned to maximum. A microphone is suspended inside a Saudi oil tanker as it fills with oil. As we hear the throb and gush of it rush over us, some recordings fade in taken inside windowless trucks in the rain, carrying animals to abattoirs. Office staff are hiding under tables while we listen to muffled shouting. Someone quietly pulls a needle out of the arm of a heroin addict; we may not even hear this. A family is trying to quietly pack all their things in a single suitcase as fast as they can before dawn breaks. We may not hear them either. A legal assistant is putting piles of A4 paperwork in to manila folders by the light of her phone. A sudden jolt and we are inside the walk-in wardrobe of the mistress of an American Republican senator listening to a Mexican cleaner sweeping up broken glass.

An exotic headpiece is pulled firmly onto the head of an actor by a wigs specialist. A film catering truck pulls into a parking lot by a river beneath the light of a full moon.

A microphone is hidden at the bottom of a basket of dirty laundry as it makes its way up some stairs on a ship, past the sound of banging from a locked metal door. A bottle of Brunello di Montalcino slips a little in its slot in a wine cellar as a helicopter goes overhead. A rat nibbles the corner of a cardboard box of old contracts in the attic of a building on Rue de Varenne in Paris. A radio controlled Subaru BRAT drives slowly up a driveway. A woman is unconscious by stairs, but we hear her breathing. A chef is trying to finely slice a tomato by the light of his phone, but slices through his thumb instead.

Someone in the costume department is steaming a peasant's outfit. A crew member is rigging a bank of fake keyboards and various bits of music technology on a vast stage.

A photography student slips a photo of Eric Garner into a chemical bath in a school darkroom. Someone is standing on the rim of a toilet bowl in the dark in a toilet cubicle quietly counting poker chips over the sound of flushing. A volunteer at a cancer-charity shop picks up a box dumped by the door full of golliwog toys and t shirts with racist slogans on. A girl rattles her piggy bank as her father turns the lights out at bedtime. It's answered by every child awake with a piggy bank at home, rattling theirs in response. Someone has recorded all the individual clicks of computer mice used in the planning, making and editing of the new Marvel film and played them one after another at extremely high speed. A coin falls off the top of an overflowing vegan café tips jar. A furious clattering of trains race round tiny tracks as a model-railway enthusiast with his house lights off bends down at eye level and watches the tiny red and green lights on the trains as they whizz round too fast. A jackhammer attacks a pavement, recorded out of the window of an ad agency office nearby. A hard drive spins, writing picture and movie data – we hear it from a contact mic placed inside the housing. A ball bearing bounces down the stairs of a dolls' house at midnight. Someone hurls a collection of VHS tapes from the top floor of a tower block just as the street lights turn on.

Beneath artificially bright lights, next to a huge fake waterfall, a laying of fake gold plates on a golden tablecloth. An injection of chemicals into a body.

An Olympic sprinter is slowly pulling on Lycra at night. A worker is raking already-rotten leaves from the cover of an outdoors swimming pool sealed for winter. We listen from the perspective of a plastic diver toy bobbing on the surface below. Warm coconut oil is being dripped onto the back of a DJ having a massage in a São Paulo hotel bedroom. Now we're inside the throat of a heavy smoker, hearing the peculiar rasp of phlegm. Someone who's overslept and missed their alarm is snoring loudly. An underpaid teenager is washing dishes out of sight at a private members' club. A footballer is pumping iron too quickly in a home gym. Rupert Murdoch bangs his hand on a table. Now we hear the turn of the mechanical coat rack in the cloakroom of the Royal Academy of Arts in Piccadilly. A Lazy Susan in a Thai restaurant is pushed round agitatedly by a waiter. Now we're inside a diamond mine. Now inside a bag of Christmas decorations in an Ohio garage, a faded Santa starts to make the sounds of Christmas, but its batteries are low and it sounds like a distorted, pitchless growl. Now we're inside the body of an upright piano in Venice. A man shouts at a woman: we can't hear the words, but the piano's lower strings are vibrating in sympathy. We're now in a coffin listening to earth being shovelled on top in long, slow clumps. A small boat rounds the headland at dawn.

A young boy is wearing ill-fitting boots and a woollen cap from a bygone era and is stamping to keep himself warm. Twelve sky-divers are waiting for the signal to jump and are gently punching each other on the arms as a gesture of support in the same rhythm as the boy.

A shovel of coal into a boiler. An aerobics class is struggling to keep up with the teacher. A wine exporter is having an affair in a car park. Someone goes over a waterfall inside a barrel. A girl drops her newly extracted bloody tooth on the top floor of a bus. A journalist has a virtual-reality headset on, but it seems to be broken. As she twists her head, we can hear she is struggling to breathe. An Egyptian man is tied to a chair, shivering, with an eye mask on. We hear a kettle boiling in the background. A drone pilot is hyperventilating in the bathroom at a friend's barbeque. A dead pigeon is frozen in ice, by a river, but a microphone is frozen alongside it and we hear the studs in motorbike tyres over the top at the same pace as the shovels of earth on the coffin lid. Several plumbers are on their backs using ratchets trying to unblock something untoward and you can hear the quick click click click of the ratchet as they unscrew the pipes. A classic-car garage is respraying a damaged car. A fisherman has fallen overboard at night and is drowning in the darkness. A craftsperson is weaving a pot from human hair. Someone with an unsteady hand is making a scale replica of a Nazi-occupied French village and from a micro-phone placed in the model of the local church, we hear the brief whirr of an electric screwdriver. A musician in Tehran has put a microphone inside a crash helmet and is tapping the outside of it with a pair of car-battery clamps to try and get a decent kick-drum sound out of it. It becomes boomy and works for a while, even though the rhythm is uneven and out of time. A huge oil barrel tips over in a car forecourt in Port-au-Prince and glugs down a drain in the gaps between the helmet taps. The roar of a steel blast furnace. Drawers full of screws, bolts, nuts and nails come crashing down. A video-game sound designer has too-dark sunglasses on and has smoked too much weed but is still trying to replicate the sound of a black hole for a documentary on the solar system.

A sound recordist on set has the hiccoughs and is holding up filming on a set. A lighting rigger is swinging from a harness up in the gantry in a partially built Olympic stadium; we hear the creak of the harness.

A woman is sewing the lining into someone else's handbag. A phone is ringing in the bottom of an abandoned wire basket in a shop during a power cut. A stuntwoman about to ride a horse off a cliff into a river is pulling on ropes in a sharp, jagged rhythm. The singer from your favourite contemporary band is breathing a little faster than usual. Someone is pulling off used sheets from a bed. A clicking together of two bits of metal at an arms factory in one satisfying clunk. An official stamp on a stained piece of paper. A tailor squatting down picks through a box of safety pins. A black Mercedes car door closes quietly. An orgasm. A doctor is picking scabs off an arm.

A gay cheerleader troop is in the middle of a warm-up routine somewhere outside of America. A special FX person is priming an explosion.

The smash of skittles as a pharmacist on a night out in a bowling alley gets a strike and then a huge crashing and shattering of glass is made up of many sounds piled up on top of each other: a teenager kicking a bin really hard in a rehearsal room in Wales, spilling bottles of Coke and non-alcoholic beer everywhere; a stunt person throwing themselves through the window of a fake corporate law firm; a chandelier falling from the ceiling of a European theatre by accident; an actor hurling a wine glass at a wall, but we don't know if it's part of the show or backstage; a movie extra punching one of the light bulbs round the outside of a mirror; a fruit bowl being knocked off a table in a Portuguese recording studio; a body smashing through the windscreen of a car on a film set in Hong Kong; the glass from a pair of glasses being ground into the wooden planks of an opera-house stage.

A sound person is fixing a microphone to the neck brace of an actor dressed as a slave and we hear her tapping on the mic as she does it. A prop-maker takes a swig of fake beer and spits it in a nearby plant pot at the moment the tapping stops.

A child is peeling off mouldy wallpaper. A child is climbing through a small black hole. A child is climbing onto the top of a train. A child is picking up a loaded gun. A child is shaking a sealed jigsaw box. A child is drinking bleach. A child is doing their homework. A child is clinging on to its parent's back in a river. A child is falling backwards off a ladder. A child is flipping pancakes. A child is turning a torch on. A child is reading a book about child labour during the industrial revolution. A child is picking food out of a bin. A child is picking fruit. A child is in a quarry. A child is sorting out shellfish in a bucket. A child is on the back of a moped with his two sisters. A child is tending a bonfire of toxic waste. A child is eating a hot dog. A child is stealing a wallet in a train station. A child is making shoes. A child is drawing a picture of a bomb exploding. A child is dressing up as Darth Vader. A child is running across the road. A child is smoking something other than a cigarette. A child is throwing a toy penguin in the air again and again. A child is making a prison from Lego. A child is walking through the door to piano lessons. A child is walking towards a crowd wearing an explosives belt. A child is throwing peanuts to peacocks. A child is crying on a train station platform, having missed their train. A child is pulling pages out of a diary and screwing them up. A child is holding the hands of their mother very tightly. A child is on their father's shoulders, playing his head like it was a pair of bongos. A child is restlessly trying to get to sleep. A child is slamming a door closed. A child is dipping a candle in wax. A child is running for the door. A million children are now running towards a door. The child of the worker by the crane is asleep in a different country.

The whirr of fans on high-wattage studio lights in a TV studio in Florida. Singers are calling their agents on the phone but not getting through.

The buzzer to talk to security in a car park. A door buzzer in Montreal. Another buzzer to a clinic in Reykjavik. All the buzzers to prison gates, to gated communities, to nightclubs, to illicit poker games. A milkman knocks on your door and an accountant slams his laptop shut in anger. At that exact moment, we hear all the estate agents opening doors to prospective buyers right now in a cascade of roads and room tones and birds and footsteps and shouts and planes and TVs and kettles. A churning inside all the cash machines spewing money out. A cacophony of printers, one in each major city in every country in the world printing out legal documents in cases between corporations and governments. It's a torrent of clatter and ink. From that dense clustering of noise comes a new cacophony, the voluminous rattle and metallic shiver of millions of coat hangers tumbling out of boxes on the floor of clothes retailers across Europe and North America. From that cacophony comes the high-speed *furr* of money-counting machines in all the banks knowingly and unknowingly processing laundered cash from drug cartels. From that mechanical fluttering to the sound of billions of white tablets made by pharmaceutical companies in India skittering through stainless-steel grading and sorting machines. Millions of robots are building things right now. From this to the sound of everyone in the finance industry at their desk right now typing the word 'money' in an email. To all the coins tipped into parking meters. From this to the world's photo-copiers on full. After this we hear everyone doing a marketing presentation right now using a pen on a whiteboard. Those millions of tiny squeaks segue into all the builders drilling into the walls of people who've bought their houses with borrowed money, and then into all the architects taking photos right now of building plots or sites on their mobile phones, then into all the journalists driving too fast towards a story, then into all the airline-industry personnel brushing and styling their hair right now in preparation to meet passengers, into all the insurance companies stapling photocopied documents together right now, into all the bleeps made by all the computers in call centres right now, into all the warning alarms in all the stockrooms and warehouses right now, into all the mouse clicks right now, into all the people programming computers right now, into all the scanning of barcodes right now, into all the volunteers at charity organisations shaking money-collection tins right now. All the consultants and managers and freelancers drying their hands in a corporate bathroom right now, into all the writers paying for a coffee right now, into all the musicians taking their instruments out of their cases, into all the TV crews setting up, into all the doctors coughing right now, into all the fashion designers cutting cloth right now, into all the clogs on floorboards, into all the people making odd noises in their sleep in labs, into all the madeleines in trays sliding into ovens, into all the people collecting eggs, into all the people knitting, into all the receptionists putting on headsets or headphones right now, into all the people combing lice out of pets' fur now, into all people in advertising sitting back in a comfy chair right now. All the drivers climbing out of their cabs, cars and trucks, to all the social- and care-service workers carrying a tray right now with someone else's food on, to all the physios and fitness instructors warming down about now, to all the body-guards and security people having a shower right now, to all the soldiers dragging on a cigarette right now, to all the porn stars getting dressed right now, into all the farmers closing gates right now.

A mobile recording studio is putting on a fan heater in a recording booth in preparation for an actor to do a voiceover on a dramatisation about an invisible workforce in Qatar. A producer is throwing pens at a wall.

At dawn, the worker by the crane drops his yellow hard hat on the floor with all the others and then heads to a bus to take him back to the accommodation block.

All the applause happening right now, everywhere in the world, played at once.

A roar of approval at an awards ceremony. A bar full of musicians drinking.

10.

Rubato

To be naked

It is dark: pitch-black, no light in front, very little behind or to either side. You would struggle to see your own flesh. Initially it feels like the darkness hums, but the more still you are, you realise it probably doesn't, although you can't be entirely sure. From somewhere on your right-hand side comes the distant sound of what you imagine to be hot water rushing through a pipe. The pipe is buried beneath the floor, but it doesn't sound like a particularly big pipe. Soon the rushing stops. Something is cooling down and metal is ticking. On the left, something in the room next door settles itself – a boiled kettle, maybe. Someone is unzipping something very slowly, very quietly. A rustle of stiff cotton slightly to the right. You begin to notice the blood throbbing a little in your ears. Then someone walks slowly towards you. You can hear leather soles on the fibres of the carpet. The tiny sound of a single unbuttoning. The microphone has been placed right next to the ear and we are hearing this button slipping through cotton, close up, in intense, excruciating detail. The gentle twisting-off of a plastic top. A wet razor along skin. Oil slipping between fingers. There is the sound of shortened breath by your ear. The creak of wood on a chair. Maybe the faraway sound of an aeroplane high overhead. A hand slips over nylon. A curtain tugged sideways gently to hide the smallest chink of light creeping in. Someone swallows. The muffled sound of a TV bleeding through the wall as it seems to play a series of sixteen very short documentaries on a loop. Breathing, shallower than before. Another unbuttoning. The drop of a shoe to the floor from a short height. The palm of a hand gently face down on a table. The picking up of a wine glass followed immediately by a tiny chink of teeth on the glass as it meets the lips. A wooden creak again. Liquid settles in a glass. To your left, a resettling of clothes on the floor. In your right ear, a wetness, possibly a mouth. A kiss. A door ajar. The running of water. In your left ear, the sound of skin on skin. A shift – the sound of bare feet on marble. Someone else swallows. A different breath in each ear. Then bare feet on warm, wet marble, just three steps. A bed sheet pulled slowly across a bed. A finger rocking lightly on a switch but not activating it. The spit of wax on a wick as it catches. A tongue separates from the roof of a mouth. An in-breath. An arrangement of hair. A tiny catching of fibres on a naked heel. A dilation, elastic. The ring of metal. A glass bottle placed gently on a floor. Someone swallows. The water stops. An in-breath in your left ear, three drips of distant water in your right. You notice your own breath brushing past the hairs inside your nose. You may be able to hear a raised heart-beat, or blood passing rapidly behind your ears. The soft crease of leather. The sound of a small crack of wood on the chair. The hinge of a door. The hushed creak of a parting limb as it's bent at a joint. The scrunch of springs under weight. The soft rhythms of skin. The wetness of a mouth. The long slip of flesh. The bristling of hair. The idling of blood.

11.

Moderato

To synthesize

It's not yet light and an alarm goes off in Kelebija on a waterproof digital watch resting on a small pile of paperwork in a plastic folder. A teacher turns off the alarm and, slowly waking up, tries not to disturb her family sleeping next to her.

Elsewhere someone begins to pull on the end of a roll of Sellotape. We can hear it being pulled out very slowly, stretched. As it unravels, it also warps and twists but mixed in such a way that we still hear the original dry sound underneath. It sounds initially like the person is about to wrap a present, but the pulling of the tape doesn't stop, it just keeps going and going. From the quality of the noise, the person is clearly trying to create as even a sound as possible, a continual unsticking and separating of the tape from the roll. The mic is slowly moving away from the source of the tape. We begin to realise the tape is likely to continue much longer than we would expect. The sound of the tape itself is getting quieter. This lasts roughly 459 seconds, until the whole roll is undone. By the time we get to the end, the microphone is with the unwound tape but far from the end of the roll in the person's hand. By this point we have also heard and worked out that there is someone else nearby who is doing their best to be quiet. Their job is to deal with all the sticky tape itself as it peels away from the roll. From the quiet sticky shuffle we can imagine piles of tape on the floor, stuck together in awkward patterns and clumps, impossible to put back on the roll. We hear the tape come to a stop with a muffled, mini jolt and at that moment, torrential rain starts falling on a bus roof in Turkey.

The teacher is now cleaning her teeth in a crude plastic bowl in the corner.

Now the stereo image opens out in a huge landscape. There are 195 teachers, one in each country, starting to unravel rolls of Sellotape in the same continuous fashion as the first person. They pull the tape from a roll attached to a microphone stand; they are now walking backwards, heading precisely in the direction of the single person who is responsible for the largest amount of the world's pollution.

The rest of the teacher's family in Kelebija are still asleep as she zips closed her toiletries bag in an even motion near them.

Over the top of the peeling Sellotape, we hear the following human-made noises played out of a number of secondary- or high-school public-address systems.

The nasty, motorised growl of a Nespresso machine. A rabbi slicing crusty bread.

The strange non-pitched growling bleep of reversing bulldozers atop a landfill site. A politician's electric toothbrush vibrating on a granite worktop.

The crunch of a broken plastic seed tray underfoot. The wheezy *crunk* of a plastic water bottle uncrunching itself. A vibrator.

A Maersk container ship bumping into a harbour wall as it docks. The hum of a predator drone mic'ed from the ground in Pakistan.

A bleep from a radio inside an abandoned police car. An answer of every bleep from the lifts in every building over eighteen storeys in London.

A parent pumping up a bike tyre. The fall of two-pence pieces in a machine in the Flamingo games arcade in Margate.

An old golf ball hit. A new car door swung open.

A lighting of incense. The flame of a Bunsen burner.

A senior member of a royal family flushes the toilet. The ping of a small stone from under the metal rim of a ceremonial carriage down the Mall.

The brushing of a half-buried skull by an archaeologist. A coach carrying a school's rugby team pulls in next to a line of waiting parents.

Every American flag in the rain. The *tang tang tang* on the metal masts in the wind at a sailing school.

A metal detector on a beach in Chile. A flipping of the pages of an Argos catalogue.

Many brides down many church aisles. A field recording of Bashar al-Assad's head hitting the pillow in preparation to sleep.

Seventy people rubbing credit cards together. An elderly couple driving to a voting station.

An osteopath clicks the neck of a retail manager. All the library books that are open right now suddenly closing together.

All the people writing letters. All the bones rattling in anonymous graves.

People digging a hole. People wrapping a present.

Someone exhausted cutting roses in a greenhouse. Every heart beating faster than normal.

The gun at the start of a marathon for charity. A glass of water put on a $200,000 table.

A black man cooking another black man dinner. The gush of marble fountains.

Everyone buying something. A missile launch.

The metallic swipe that accompanies every use of a blade in a film, even though it made no noise in real life. The sound of a group of extras on a film set trying to dance quietly but excitedly even though there's no music on in the background.

The drop of tablets into glass trays. The slip of Prince Charles's skin against a woman's arm.

The wrapping of a body in a blanket. The boarding queue of a low-cost airline.

The *clunk hiss* of every can of Coca-Cola in Colombia being opened at the same time. The ring of Roger Ames's mobile phone on an overly polished mahogany dresser.

An ambulance driving over a speed bump. The bang of a swing bin in the ladies' toilet at the headquarters of a pharmaceutical company.

The head of a dead refugee bumping loosely against the side of a lorry, as yet undiscovered. The sound just after all the air conditioning is turned off at the *Daily Mail*.

A strong, hot shower directly onto the head of a bald man. A leakage from an industrial petrochemical plant.

The grind of an African stone mill in a recreation of a scene shown in the Powell Cotton Museum. The setting down of a tray of alcoholic cocktails at an open-air bar in a hotel in Bahrain.

The pop of a light bulb blowing. The opening of a box of protein snack bars.

The shimmer of shopping trolleys. Every boat sinking together.

The poke of a straw into a giant cup of Mountain Dew. The dropping of a large spanner in the maintenance room of a hospital.

The small flicker of sticky noise made after having applied lipstick as someone parts their lips. Two thousand hotel doors slammed shut.

Part of the sound of someone being stoned to death. Part of a car wash.

A forest uprooted. The squeal of a dog chew toy.

The tick of keys on a keyboard as someone types a complaint. A recreation of the sound of the building at Rana Plaza collapsing made by a musician using mainly coat hangers and security tags stolen from Primark stores.

A packet of free nuts on a train sliding across a plastic table at speed. Someone drawing the curtains before another night of abuse.

The loading of a crossbow. The buzzer marking the end of a student basketball game.

A cathode-ray TV set turning on. The stapling of a stomach in a cosmetic surgery operation.

The telephone wake-up call from a hotel's front desk. The kiss on a child's head.

A breaking leg slowed down significantly so we hear the fibres tear and snap. A plane taking off heard in the background while someone is printing an article about voter disenfranchisement in Ohio.

The pulling out of a tooth with string attached to a large rock thrown over a cliff. A cream applied to a rash on someone else's back.

Wire cutters on a chain-link fence. Murky water in a swimming pool lapping at the underside of an inflatable pool animal.

A safe lock being picked. A child's black nylon tie being put on by an adult.

A brief summary of weddings, parties, funerals and births through a hood and ear muffs. A general sips rum.

The spit of eggs and bacon in a pan. The noises of a CT scanner.

A forest fire set by arson. A waterfall of Lego.

A thin plastic stirrer for tea plucked by a bored child. A million pieces of disposable cutlery tipped down the chimney of a country house.

Football studs in a tunnel. A police taser.

A handful of olives thrown down the toilet in room 720 in Moscow Park Inn. Every stuffed animal from a hospital flown from kites.

A killer whale bangs against bars. A leather baseball on a window, but it doesn't break.

The creak of windows in Hungarian hotels. The dropping of a can of Red Bull at a prehistoric monument.

An artist writing with chalk on a blackboard a brief description of the imagined sound of all the plugs simultaneously being pulled out of unused baths. An excerpt of someone assembling a wardrobe in entirely the wrong way.

The empty train carriage 006 waiting to leave Saint Petersburg station. A goth in a river, head under water, stroking the outside of her ears.

The sound of cancer cells reproducing unheard in the body of someone going swimming at dawn. The creak of an antique floorboard as someone tiptoes across it in the dark.

The hammering of a large fence post. The smashing of a radio with a spade.

A cicada on the pillar of a temple in Kyoto. Tights being pulled up.

A coin in a wishing well. A bedspring compacted.

The edited sound of a huge block of luxury flats being built from scratch, sped up so that from breaking ground to fully occupied takes just fifteen seconds. Poker chips being organised into piles.

Prawn balls, just out of the fryer in a Chinese takeaway in Frankfurt, settling at the bottom of a polystyrene cup. An office chair spins against the corner of a desk.

A soldier coming straight through a door without opening it. The slide of a grubby beige computer mouse on a Homer Simpson mouse mat.

The crackle of plastic around a tampon. The robbing of a bank.

The boiling of sugar in huge vats. The slip of rope against the skin of 13,000 necks.

A time-stretch of all the food in a chain of themed restaurants going rotten. A drag on a menthol cigarette.

Every scream happening right now.

The Sellotape stops.

The teacher's family are now awake and are lining up together with others. One of the children is wearing headphones. A bird sings, a truck passes and uses its horn in a long, unpleasant blast. We hear it recorded from a mic set on top of a tower some distance away. The adults shuffle forward.

Wind passes through holes in a wall with an eerie sound. A man in uniform is starting to run.

One by one, each sound now played from all the outside speakers that usually play music or announcements, such as those at sports stadiums or those attached to red-brick walls of Frankie & Benny's restaurants, or from the tops of mosques, or racetracks, or drive-in cinemas, or train stations, or ferry ports, or landing docks, or loading bays, or town centres, or part of giant screens in Shibuya. From grey, nasal-sounding speakers at village fêtes, or along the finishing lines to city marathons. At the Mexican border, or at night markets, or at Israeli checkpoints, or hi-tech advertising billboards, or at petrol stations, or at free parties in the woods, or Brazilian carnivals, or car forecourts, or at protest rallies, or school sports days. From the tops of tanks, or near ski lifts, or suspended from helicopters, or at fairgrounds, or as torture into shipping containers, or on Ibiza beaches, or from the top deck of a politician's bus as it drives past, we hear: All the hotel washing machines churning away right now, all the hikers hiking upwards, everyone eating crisps right now, all the ferries leaving port, all the phones ringing, all the showers running, all the fires in grates in houses, all the cable cars setting out, every text message received right now, all the joggers on treadmills, all the pans on stoves, all the cheers at fascist rallies, all the swimmers in rivers, all the industrial fires, all the people opening bills, tearing paper, all the toilets flushing, all the cutlery on all the plates at the ends of meals, all the beer from pumps, all the silent debt, all the typing of racist or misogynist comments on keyboards right now, all the papers in exams being turned over at once, all the guard dogs barking, all the escalators going up, all the burglar alarms going off, all the light aircraft lining up, all the chicken being fried, all the cremulators grinding down human remains to ash, everyone getting dressed for a christening, someone your age walking towards danger, all the hair being cut, all the contactless bleeps in shops and at train turnstiles, all the football games about to start, all the getting undressed, all the tractors reversing, all the hockey sticks being loaded into changing rooms, all the popping of knees out of joints, all the children dropped off at school, all the train doors closing, all the punches landing on faces, all the sewing machines, all the air conditioning in courtrooms, all the patients on beds on the move down hospital corridors, all the peeling-off of wallpaper by builders, all the leather soles on wet stones, all the bricks thrown through windows, many copies of this book burning, all the trees being felled with chainsaws, all the suitcases clicking open, all the printing of lobbyists' business cards, all the dancers in dance studios in South America warming up without music, all the babies breastfeeding, all the social workers ringing doorbells or pushing buzzers, all the tinned prunes peeled open, all the speedboat engines revving, all the whistles from owners to their dogs, all the overdoses, all explosion sound effects being auditioned in film suites, all the cheers at a pub quiz on hearing the answer to a difficult question, all the loudest people shouting, all the apples being eaten at once right now, all the chefs sharpening knives, all the shivering. All the people unfolding large stiff maps outside in the wind, all the cleaning of windows, all the people about to jump off cliffs or mountains with flying things on their backs, all the water fountains, all the men about to commit rape. All the people climbing ladders, all the people digging holes, all the planting of trees in shopping malls, all the coughing from air pollution, all the people in factories making things they can't afford to buy themselves, all the pumping of chemicals into fracking boreholes, all the heaters at the entrances to shops, all the plastic things melting in fires, all the flies on corpses, all the cracking of rotten walnuts, all the people pumping the chests of other people whose hearts have stopped, all the desperate writers in rooms, all the slashing of skin with knives. All the chains, all the locks, all the metal bars, all the lawyers, all the journalists, all the bars of chocolate snapped. All the crying, all the tears of disbelief, all the weeping into hands, all the sobbing in showers, all the tearful faces raised to the sky. All the anger, all the violent shuddering, all the people in queues, at checkpoints, being searched, stopped by police unnecessarily. All the fish being caught in ponds and rivers. All the baking of birthday cakes. All the sticking-up of posters to gigs. All the breaking of rocks. All the waste, the mess, the excess, the rubbish, the bins, the bending, the burying, the burning. All the people running. All the people opening curtains. All the rowing boats setting out on lakes. All the people getting into taxis to a party. All the people putting on their wedding outfits. All the people passing an exam. All the people reading the last page of a book. All the people bounding downstairs, shouting with joy.

All the people reaching land

All the people coming up for air

All the new babies

All the keys in doors to new houses

All the perfect presents being opened

All the traffic lights turning green

All the people throwing a stick for their dog

All the people laughing at different jokes

All the champagne pops

All the needles on all the records

All the people sinking into hot baths after a long day

All the people on their knees smiling with their ear to the ground

All the people listening to someone else about to tell a story

All the people taking a bite of a piece of ripe, fresh fruit they just picked from a tree

All the children on roller skates

All the adults about to go out into the cold, putting on a warm coat

All the children in slavery suddenly free

All the curtains going up in theatres

All the plants growing in unlikely places

Everyone who's getting paid properly for their time and work waking up

Everyone who is just about to win something amazing hearing a knock at the door

Everyone stepping onto a fairground ride

All the actors walking on stage

Everyone making a meal for someone else at home

Every person who escaped on foot from the cruel state apparatus of a tyrant

Every campfire catching

All the people humming nonsense under their breath
Every child making it across a road safely
All the caramel bubbling
Every person who got through a day without a racist
    incident putting on a kettle
All the bands about to play the first note of a gig
All the kisses of lovers
All the wild applause and cheering happening right now
All the tea pickers in China having a day off
All the people being pulled alive from the sea
All the people going on holiday
All the people held unjustly being released from prison
All the high fives with children
All the hurdles cleared, ditches jumped, javelins thrown
All the items just collected in lost property
All the people reunited at airports holding each other
    tightly
All the people about to dive into a pool
All the pets meeting their owners at the door
All the removals lorries pulling into a new drive
All the gymnasts landing a complicated trick
All the women graduating from university
All the subsistence farmers collecting a bumper harvest
All the skateboarders not falling off
All the people spotting a rare bird
All the orgasms
Everyone on a plane to meet a new grandchild
Everyone buying their first history book
Everyone loading a DVD into a machine
Everyone casting their vote
Every person standing in front of a bulldozer
Everyone signed off by a doctor
Everyone paying off debts
Every murderer caught
Every unjust lawsuit suddenly thrown out
Everyone sitting down to dinner with the love of their life
Every peaceful gathering of a democratic movement
Every woman in danger making it to a refuge

Everyone poor finding a big envelope of cash
Everyone tired falling asleep
Everyone standing up in solidarity
Every nuclear weapon being dismantled
Every set of twins reunited after years apart
Everyone pressing 'play' on their first piece of finished
        recorded music
Every plane landing
Every handshake between new friends
Every glass of clean water being poured
Every doorbell with a joyful surprise on the other side
        of the door
Everyone reaching the top of a mountain
Everyone making it through security
Everyone with an umbrella putting it up as it starts to
        rain
Anyone hungry about to eat
All the people getting a job they really wanted
Every bunch of flowers handed over
Every skier setting off
Every zip of every tent
All the rattling of unused guns
All the people finally on their way home
Every despot in hiding or on the run
Everyone about to play an instrument
Everyone's heartbeat pounding in unison
Everyone about to break out into song
Everyone moving onto the dance floor
Everyone running towards each other
Everyone running towards each other
Everyone running towards each other
The sound of everyone running towards each other

12.

Diminuendo

The sound of an object leaving the earth. The sound of the friction between the atmosphere and the earth as it spins.

The sound of a

dense, collapsing mass

as it

hurtles

past.

The sound of a body

breaking up into its constituent parts.

The impossible sound of
solar winds.

The sound of a continuous bombardment of parti-
cles. The sound of gravity hurling a distant planet round a distant
sun. The sound of the distortion at the edges of dust. The sound
of black holes collapsing. The sound of light as it passes through

virgin space.

                        multiplying
                        multiplying
                        multiplying
                        multiplying
                        multiplying
                        multiplying
                        multiplying
                        multiplying
                        multiplying
                        multiplying
                        multiplying
                        multiplying
                        multiplying
                        multiplying
                        multiplying
                        multiplying
The sound of cells multiplying at dizzying speeds.
                        multiplying
                        multiplying
                        multiplying
                        multiplying
                        multiplying
                        multiplying
                        multiplying
                        multiplying
                        multiplying
                        multiplying
                        multiplying
                        multiplying
                        multiplying
                        multiplying
                        multiplying
                        multiplying
                        multiplying
                        multiplying
                        multiplying
                        multiplying
                        multiplying

The sound of dark energy expanding.

All the shuddering of elements.

The sound of an explosion.

Glossary

4/4 – common time signature in Western music denoting four
    beats to each bar

AM (amplitude modulation) – type of radio signal

audio spectrum – range of sonic frequencies

binaural recording – recording made with two microphones,
    to simulate the precise audio image heard by human ears

boundary-type microphone – omni-directional microphone
    mounted on a flat surface

bpm – beats per minute

CDR – CD that can be recorded to on a one-time basis

choke – valve to restrict air flow to a car engine

circuit-bent drum machine – drum machine that's been hacked
    or modified

contact mic – microphone physically touching the thing it wishes
    to record

crossfade – segue between two audio files

delay – treatment of a sound that creates an artificial echo of
    the original

digital distortion – corruption of a digital audio file

downbeat – first beat of the bar

DPA mic – manufacturer often associated with small
    microphones worn on TV or film sets

EQ – short for equalisation, adjusting the tone of a sound

frequency spectrum – see *audio spectrum*

FX – synonym for special effects

high-pass filter – filter that removes lower frequencies

hydrophone – microphone for recording in fluids, usually water

Hz – unit measurement for hertz, the unit measurement of
    frequencies

kick drum – also known as bass drum, the largest drum in a
drum set played with the foot, now associated with drum
machines

laid in – mixed within

Lomo shotgun mic – Russian-made microphone, used to record
from a distance

loop (v.) – to repeat a section of music

metal-plate reverb – made famous by German company, EMT,
an effect that creates the impression of a room or space by
passing sound through a metal plate

mix value – control function to allow you to mix between
untreated audio and the chosen effect

omni microphone – microphone that can record in all directions
at once

overlay (v.) – to lay on top of

pitch-shifter – change the pitch of a sound

reverb – the effect of sound within a space

reverb tail – end of the reverb part of a sound wave

ribbon microphone – microphone that uses an electro-magnetic
ribbon to capture sound

room-simulation reverb – a technique to remotely simulate the
sound of specific spaces

semitone – the smallest interval in Western classical music

shotgun microphone – microphone used to record from a
distance

sound image (page 65 stereo image, and other places) –
the complete audible landscape of a recording

sub rumble – cluster of particularly low frequencies

tape delay – delay effect created with a tape loop

transient (n.) – the peak of an audio wave, usually at the start

vamp (n.) – musical phrase that loops indefinitely until the music
or musicians are ready to move on to the next section

volume ride – moving the fader to allow for amplitude changes

Sounds the supporters heard
as they were pledging to
help publish this book

The hum of air conditioning, the ticking of a wall clock, typing sounds on my laptop, inner murmur of my anxieties and insecurities about an upcoming performance and about life in general, air conditioning, speaker explaining 3D printing methods (bit of an echo), shuffling and the general sound of people being quiet. Metal chairs being shifted around, children sounding out words, occasional beeps by ATM machines and cash registers, birds that accidentally flew into the building panic-chirping as they try to figure out how to escape, a fountain, the hum of invisible air conditioners, gangs of college students and aspiring novelists seated around me turning pages quietly, the sounds of the mobile phone used by a lone medical worker dressed in his scrubs. Every sound echoes in the building because of all the metal and glass, so the distant sounds cannot be distinguished at times. It's all very three dimensional. The crackle of my old plastic water bottle as I take a long drink, the slight vibration and tap of my phone keyboard and the distant echo of voices two floors below me as they make their way up the disabled lift shaft. Occasional wind bursts, rattling leaves in the treetops. Sunbathing neighbour turning pages in a magazine. Paul Kalkbrenner beats and aeroplane noise. The fan on my computer. In the distance, a car. (It might be a car.) The JMZ train, air conditioner, street traffic, my legs shifting around as I lay in bed reading, a construction site, salsa and reggaeton. I hear now the tic tac and the clock of my ancient watch at the wall of my veranda and a car from far away, a documentary on the sea, so crashing waves, and passing trains, and my wife typing, the hum of machines (refrigerator, laptop fan), bird chirps, crickets, tree leaves rustled by the wind, boat engines from a distance, an extractor fan humming while old pipes refill a cistern, distant traffic drowned by intermittent vehicles and muted discussions passing by, heavy breathing, chuckling and gentle tapping on phones, interspersed by the occasional fart, cat litter being cleaned, city humming, hard disc rolling, computer fans working, keyboard being used, I can hear the sound of people walking on the beach, talking with one ear and the muffled sound of water breaking on the shore with the other, I am laying down on a beach in Spain, seagulls and tinnitus, the fan of my laptop, my cervical vertebrae, a bus passing, the clock of the city hall (two o'clock), a motorbike screaming down the street, the water tank dripping in the loft above me and a child singing in a garden across the way, the sound of my hands on this keyboard, I can hear voices of my little sons, they are playing at the swimming pool, it is the most beautiful sound I've ever heard, digital squirrels leaking from the attic, my own typing, a blend of laptop fan, remote noises of cars going by (indirectly, being reflected from the other side of the building) and light wind in an otherwise very quiet surrounding, myself typing, computer fan, birds sing-ing, distant road noises, Barry Stoller's Match of the Day theme performed by an ice-cream van, accompanied by passing car bass and the ever-present whir of my laptop fan, with my right ear I can hear the muffled rumble of traffic on the A444 as it passes by the front of my house, along with the vague rattling of the combine harvester in the field opposite, my left ear is being treated to the low-pitched whine and running water of the washing machine, the scrape of brushstrokes as my newly graduated stepson works on his illustration portfolio, the occasional raucous call of next-door-but-one's peacock and the sound of some sort of power tool in the goat field and suddenly a skein of geese are honking above, low, constant whirring of a dehumidifier upstairs, occasional vehicles passing on the road outside the window, my wife scratch-ing her arm (muffled by a dressing gown) on the couch next to me, my daughter laughing at unintelligible American voices on YouTube from the next room, I can hear the sound of my fingers hitting the keyboard in the empty living room, the tiny drone from the fan inside my laptop, muffled music playing inside a car waiting at the traffic light. The rattling sound of the bus's engine stopping right in front of my apartment, horns, bells from the bus, the tinnitus hissing in my left ear, the refrigerator purring in the kitchen, my neighbour's footsteps up above, it all sounds very loud and busy, but it's actually a very quiet Saturday evening, the neighbours coming up the communal stairwell, the rain against the window, cars and scooters driving on wet roads, and the hum of my crappy record player, the whirr of my desk fan, the hum of my PC and the occasional rumble as a late-night motorist crosses the bridge over the lake, computer noise, mouse clicks, keyboard key press, fan spinning, beeps, cable plug in, in and out, one cat purring, one laptop humming, two clocks ticking almost exactly half a second apart, a hard disk spinning, the sound of a helicopter passing overhead and a police car's siren on a nearby street, probably in the aftermath of a day charged with tension between police, right-wing hooligans whose 'March of the Patriots' had been declared too risky and therefore cancelled by the city, and the left-wing counter-protesters who had gathered nevertheless, as I write this the sound of fireworks, celebrating another one of our city's touristic events, this time a parade of cruise ships in the local harbour, my dog crunching and grinding a bone in his bed while traffic whizzes by outside, Channel 4 programme on TV about OCD cleaners facing down their demons, rib-eye steak, mushrooms, tomatoes, onions and Marsala cooking on the hob, poorly maintained sash windows rattling, foxes in the garden making blood-curdling sounds (probably mating), highlights of an England v Pakistan test match playing in the other room, iPhone 6 Plus key tones as I type, loud snapping in my head as I bite through my own fingernail, a faint clock ticking, a motorbike passing outside, creaks, the wind in trees outside, an aeroplane overhead, after taking off from Heathrow moments earlier; the occasional hammer-tap of Jeff (or is it Geoff?) fixing the front bedroom window; the yelp of a dog and the wind stirring autumn leaves, another plane, regular as clockwork, the DVD player is humming ever so slightly, my phone keys are tapping with every letter I write, my tummy just gurgled with hunger, something is happening outside – maybe a lawn mower in the distance or a gentle stream of traffic, a plane just flew overhead but a little way away as it wasn't very loud, the fridge humming, a small dog barking, Kevin McCloud discussing the building of a floating house, the gentle whooshing hum of a dishwasher, people discussing projects in hushed tones and Lou Reed's 'Perfect Day' playing faintly on the office stereo, the background hum of an air-conditioning unit, office colleagues talking, typing (via computer keyboards), a coin being dropped, the ping of a Blackberry, general background electronic hum, telephone hold music, droning monotonous business conversation and many hands typing, steam whooshing, ladies laughing, teaspoons clipping, the dull roar of a busy road, the jazzy, snazzy blur of background radio, creaky floorboards, squeaky hinges, dogs barking, rowdy mopeds, the dull hum of the M3, the radio playing some music, a plane flying overhead and my son playing with his toys. When it is quiet, and I am alone, after a busy and noisy day, I can sit and actually hear the rhythms of my body, the air in my lungs going in and out, the pumping of blood in and out of my heart. This, combined with tinnitus, used to frighten me, and keep me awake for hours. I then learned to accept this, and now I do acknowledge that this is a part of who I am – a deaf adult, not flawed, not even disabled really, just deaf, just Sebastian, what can I hear right now? I am in an open office at work. Everybody has gone home for their Christmas holidays. I am alone. It is bliss. The sound of the road in front of my office, a techno-like sound of a defective air conditioner in the office (I recorded it, it is really cool). DJ Sprinkles – house music is a controllable desire you can own, typing of keys on the computer, cars on Via Venezia outside the window, Ella Fitzgerald and Louis Armstrong – 'Learnin' the Blues', Mary Halvorson playing 'Sadness' by Ornette Coleman, the thud of crushing anxiety and the radiators humming with comforting warmth. My nails are too long, I am currently wearing the headphones I always wear when working on my laptop. They have active noise cancellation and as I type this I don't have any music playing so all I hear is the raspy thud of my heartbeat in my ears, birdsong, heavy rain barrelling down hard onto my office's tin roof, co-worker talking on the phone in German: '... *Ich habe jetzt schriftlich nichts dafür bekommen, aber ihren* laptop. *Ich gehe davon aus, daß alles stattfindet* ...' Footsteps from the floor above, the fan of my notebook, servers humming, numerous air-conditioning units whirring, a slight ringing, and laptop keys (obviously), air vibration, typing keyboard clicks, sounds of my

MacBook Pro computer, birds singing and road noise Chaleur Humaine by Christine and the Queens. I am deaf, so, why did I pledge to help you with your book? Speech is distorted. Music is unpleasant so I prefer to not listen to it. I wear hearing aids but these amplify everything indiscriminately, so I often leave these in, but switched off, more as a visual aid when I am in a situation where those I interact with need to know that I am deaf. Otherwise, when alone, I don't wear them at all. This is bliss.

Acknowledgements

Matthew would like to thank the people below who may regularly have made one of the following noises:

A pair of clogs on wide floorboards, some constant whistling or singing, odd gurgles of concentration, driving noises in the background of a broken conversation, the snapping of a Rich Tea biscuit in half in Exeter, the stroking of a small wiry beard, two people laughing near to Aberdeen station, the prising open of an oyster in June, standing by a roundabout in Broadstairs, cleaning a Saab in Berlin, buying U-Bahn tickets, the throwing of a log on a fire in Whitstable, the huddling round a boiling kettle in Wharf Road. And thank you to all the people who so kindly supported this book.

Unbound is the world's first crowdfunding publisher, established in 2011.

We believe that wonderful things can happen when you clear a path for people who share a passion. That's why we've built a platform that brings together readers and authors to crowdfund books they believe in — and give fresh ideas that don't fit the traditional mould the chance they deserve.

This book is in your hands because readers made it possible. Everyone who pledged their support is listed below. Join them by visiting unbound.com and supporting a book today.

Vanessa Abreu
Drew Adams
Vanessa Ainsworth
Justine Alderman
Maxime Alexandre
José Alfaro
Graham Allcott
Polly Anders
Sam Anderson
Igor Arabaolaza
Pierre Arlais
Adrian Arratoon
Jon Ashton
Simon Ashton
John Ayers
Luca Ballarini
Tiago Barros
Pete Beck
Hanna Behnke

Ludwig Berger
Dettifoss Bergmann
Pedro Bergmann
Manuela Beste
Omer Bil
Clare Birchall
Andy Birtwistle
Joseph Bleasdale
Carlos Boix
Steve Brandwood
Florian Bräunlich
Paul Briottet
Martin Brown
Ryan Bruce
Giles Bunch
Mike Burn
Mike Butcher
Adam Butler
Miguel Casas

Ben Castle
Gregory Cathcart
Heidi Chan
Jim Chancellor
Marnie Chesterton
Caroline Chignell
Liu Chong
Caryl Churchill
Tony Churnside
Federico Ciapi
John Clark
Mathew Clayton
Julian Clyne
Philip Connor
Megan Corrigan
Alex Craddock
John Cratchley
Alabaster Crippens
Jonathan Crook
Ryan Crosson
David Crozier
Drew Daniel
Rishi Dastidar
Kevin Davey
Brian Davidson
Ross Euan Davidson
Andrew Brindley Davies
Sarah De Castro
Adriaan de Roover
Simon Deacon
Kieron Deane
Tim Dellow
Leonidas Diamantis
Stephen Dillane
Wendalynn Donnan
Ben Dornan
Suzanne Dwight
Ryley Edwards

Trevor Eld
Sebastiaan Eldritch-Böersen
Christof Ellinghaus
Henrik Engström
Aurélien Estager
Alex Fiennes
Jem Finer
Sean Fitzpatrick
James Flint
Stephen France
Ben Freeney
Mike Gillespie
Nick Gilling
Matthew Gollock
Giles Goodland
David Govier
Dominic Gregory
John Griffiths
Paul Groom
Edward A Guy
Tim Hallas
Sebastian Hanusa
Matthias Hauck
Catherine Herbert
Stefan Herkenrath
Kikù Hibino
Chris Hilker
Yannick Hill
Andrew Hodgson
Ed Holloway
Stijn Hosman
Paul Howard
Nicklaus Hubben
Denis Huber
Hasan Hujairi
Kate Hutchinson
Ben Immanuel
Finbar Ishah LS

Vasil Ivanov
Graeme Jackson
Jay James
Simon W. James
Magnus Jochumsen
Lee Johnston
Alamo Jon
Hugh Jones
Nicholas Jones
Sioned Jones
Paweł Juzwuk
Keith Kahn-Harris
Alexander Kaltenbrunner
Peter Kavanagh
Dan Kieran
Otto Kokke
Peter Königsgruber
Istvan Kovari
Peter Krahn
Conrad Lambert
Matthew Lambert
Peter Lang
Carmen Lastres
Rastko Lazic
Andrew Lazonby
Emily Leather
Nancy Leawok
Gavin Leitch
Adam Lilienfeldt
Michael Lilley
Toby Litt
Chester Lusk
Guy Macdonald
Alfonso Martín Machín
Duncan Macmillan
Radim Malinic
Andy Malt
Jesse Mann

Dmitry Martov
Keith Matthews
John Matthias
Thomas Maurstad
Martine McDonagh
Vek McGuire
Ed McKeon
Andrew McMillan
David McSherry
Fidel Mehra
Anne Mensah
James Mewis
John Middleton
Andrew Milloy
Guillermo Miranda
Matthew Mirapaul
Donald Mitchell
John Mitchinson
Kenkichi Miyazaki
Jazz Monroe
Charles Morgan
Matthew Morgan
Paul Myerscough
Andrew Nairn
Murray Nance
Maurizio Narciso
Carlo Navato
Pete Nickless
Níne Líves
Ralf Nöcker
Justin O'Brien
Lola Oliyide
Ed Owen
Marcelo Panozzo
Saul Parker
Spencer Parker/Works GONDŌ
Kirk Parsons
Matthew Patterson Curry

Chris Perks
Alice Perman
Dan Peters
Rupert Philbrick
Chris Pickhaver
Justin Pollard
Dan Pope
Tim Pugh
Pedro Ramírez
Matthieu Ranc
Arun Rao
Alexis Raptopoulos
Solaris Rebula
Gordon Reilly
Lorenzo Ri
Caroline Richardson
Till Richter
James Robbins
Marius Røbech
Ross Rochford
Ralph Mortimer Roome
Steve Rose
Philip Rosenberg
Gabriel Roth
Joe Rothwell
Curtis Ruptash
Jamie Russell
Tom Ryan
Sukhdev Sandhu
Isla Sandilands
Nicolas Sartor
Marcus Sartorius
Marco Saveriano
Bernhard Schabmayr
Lennart Schalk
Régis Schneider
Chris Schrei
Alan Searl

Sebastian Seelmann
Michal Serafin
Martin Setzke
Laurence Shapiro
Marc Shearer
Cosmo Sheldrake
Sami Silden
Angel Simitchiev
Jon Slade
Mark Slicker
Ivan Smagghe
Alexis Smith
Bob Smith
Kevin Smith
Barnaby Smyth
Luke Solomon
The Stahlmann Girls
Anya Stang
Meikel Steiding
David Stevens
Pete & Catherine Stollery
G Stringer
David Surtees
Karen Sutton
Russell Swift
Ed Tanner
Jason Tar
Chris Tate
Tot Taylor
Thibault aka Anna Sound
Joshua Thomas
Tobias Thon
Panagiotis Tigas
Christian Tjaben
Koji Tsukamoto
Lorenzo Tubertini
William Vallade
Grant Janse van Rensburg

Tony Vanderheyden
Balázs Vándor
Mark Vent
Elias Vervecken
VEsound
Hugues Viardot
Ian Vine
Andrew Wales
Patrick Walsh
Dan Weiss
Robert Wells
Simon White
Krzysztof Wieczorek
Adam Williams

Jeremy Williams
Darren Winter
Susannah Wise
Anton Woldhek
Steve Woodward
John Wraight
James Wright
Alex Wybraniec
Ilya Zadokhin
Faiz Zaidi
Zilla
Bastian Zimmermann

A note about the typeface

When Le Corbuiser wrote: 'Geometry is the language of humanity', he expressed a belief that geometry was deeply human.

The typeface used in this book is Linotype Avenir. It is classified as a *humanist linear grotesque* but has its roots the geometric types of the 1920s and '30s. Designed in 1988 by the Swiss designer Adrian Frutiger (1928–2015). In a long career which spanned hot metal, phototypesetting and digital type platforms, Frutiger's influence on modern type design is difficult to overstate.

Geometric typefaces are based on the absoluteness of mathematcial perfection, on the basic forms such as circle, square and triangle, as well as linear strokes. On the other hand, a typeface – especially a text typeface – should conform to certain optical critera that render it pleasant to read. And here a contradiction rises its head. To find that balance, to recognise that moment when both aspects – the mathematical and the human – join together in equilibrium, that was for Adrian Frutiger the masterstroke in Avenir. The draughtsmanship – rather than the intellectual idea behind it – making that mathematically perfect form more pleasant to the human eye is what Mr Frutiger considered his masterpiece.

The essence of a sign is like a pure tone in music. The exterior form, however, is what makes the sound.
    – Adrian Frutiger